Red,
White, and
Dead

Heather Marie Reaves

Keeper's Press, 2019

Printed in the United States of America

First Printing, 2019

ISBN 978-0-9995199-5-0

www.hmreaves.com

For my Beloved

One

Charlie looked at the shovel propped against the porch and wished she could hit the pompous jerk in the head with it. If he called her "hon" in that condescending tone one more time, she might make her own wish come true.

Brett Clark looked like a professional wrestler. He was taller than any other man on his crew, and the only soft spot on him was the belly that hung just a little over his carpenter jeans. His tattooed arms bulged from beneath his t-shirt, and he always wore a sweat-stained Tennessee Titans cap. He was usually a laid-back kind of guy, but right now he was finding it hard to keep his temper under the brunt of Charlie's wrath.

"Listen," Charlie said, "I'm not paying you a penny more than what we've agreed on. If you can't bring this project together on the budget you agreed to, and in the timeframe you agreed to, then you and your crew can pack up your stuff right now and go home."

Brett glared at the fuming red-head. She may have inherited her grandmother's house, but she had not inherited her temperament. Betty Ann Flynn had been one of the kindest souls in Holiday Cove.

"Ms. Flynn, the delays have been unforeseen. I know this can be frustrating, but you have my word, we will be done on time even if we have to work around the clock."

Charlie took a deep breath. At least he hadn't called her "hon" this time.

"No more delays, Mr. Clark." She walked back into the rambling, pink Victorian giving Brett no time to respond.

The first floor of the mansion was cluttered with construction workers, tools, and materials. She didn't see how it would be finished within two weeks. She climbed the back staircase to the second floor where her living quarters were. At least this part of the house was complete. She heard Mr. Bear's sharp bark from the bottom of the stairs. She was running behind this morning and had not fed him his breakfast or taken him for a walk. And he was letting her know just how he felt about that.

The upstairs apartment felt cozy even though it covered the entire second floor of the mansion. Charlie had filled it with personal things from her travels, and the whole area reflected her eclectic taste. She stepped into the large living room from the foyer at the top of the stairs. Mr. Bear was in his kennel by the floor to ceiling window that overlooked the nearby old church's flower garden. He liked watching the birds and the squirrels playing in the giant oak trees. However, this morning, he only had eyes for Charlie. He watched her walk in the room, a pout on his face. His big brown eyes looked up at her, and his little underbite was sticking out. She tried not to laugh at the spoiled pooch.

"Come on, you big baby. Let's get you some breakfast before you starve to death."

She opened the kennel, and the grey ball of fluff ran to the kitchen, his little nails click-clacking on the mahogany hardwood floors. She followed after him. He waited by the pantry door, tail wagging. He ran to his food bowl and picked it up with his teeth and presented it to Charlie. She filled it with kibble and sat it back down on the floor. While the dog unceremoniously began to devour his breakfast, she filled the other bowl with fresh water and brought it back to the pantry. After she had Mr. Bear taken care of, she poured herself a cup of coffee and walked to the sun porch. This was her favorite room in the apartment. She had fond memories of having afternoon tea with her grandmother here while they watched the traffic move up and down the tiny main street. Holiday Cove was a small town nestled on a plateau in middle Tennessee, and the summer season was always busy. Lake Holiday was a popular destination, and the upcoming 4th of July holiday would bring a substantial increase in tourist dollars. It was the reason she was pushing Brett and his crew so hard. She wanted the shop downstairs open for business before the influx of out-of-towners. She took a deep breath and sat down at the small wooden breakfast table with her caramel Biscotti and a hot cup of coffee. She watched the town begin to stir as she let the coffee work its magic.

The bells of the neighboring church chimed in the eight o'clock hour. Charlie could not have asked for a better location. The pink mansion was nestled on a side street right off the main road. The old Community church took up almost the whole block to her left and reminded her of the cathedrals she had seen in Europe with the stone and wood facade topped by grand gabled roofing. The flower garden separated the two properties. The reverend had a green thumb, and vivid yellows, pinks, and reds splashed color across a canvas of lush green. A small fountain and a cafe table and chairs gave visitors a place to sit and meditate.

Across the street on the other side was Hal's Bakery. The two-story, wood-sided building was painted a pale blue with blue and white stripe awnings covering the windows and doors. Two white iron Bistro tables sat out in front. Poppy's Pet Shop with its bright yellow-colored brick flanked Hal's. Holiday Cove Realty housed in a small converted Victorian was dwarfed by the large two-story brick building that took up the rest of the space on the street and housed the Community Center.

The street behind Charlie was filled with a myriad of Victorian houses in a rainbow of colors. Some were used as residences, others for business, and some were used for

both, like Charlie's. Vic Holiday and the other founders of
Holiday Cove had constructed the houses themselves. Vic
was an architect and had fallen in love with the Victorian
homes he helped design in his time up north. After the
Depression, many of the houses had fallen in disrepair, and
Holiday Cove was becoming a ghost town. Vic's son,
Gerald saved the town in the fifties when he developed the
area around Lake Holiday. He used the money he made
from the venture to revitalize the downtown shops and
restore the Victorians. Between Lake Holiday and the new
downtown, Holiday Cove again flourished. Now, during the
summer months, many owners would allow their homes to
be part of the Historic Tours given by the Chamber of
Commerce. Through the years, the town had maintained its
charm and size while growing a thriving tourist industry.

Charlie took the last bite of Biscotti and savored the
rest of her coffee. She really shouldn't have gone downstairs
before she had her first cup. Brett probably thought she was
a shrew. Besides, he was right about her being frustrated.
He had told her from the beginning she would be better off
renting a place while the renovations were done. But she
had insisted on staying. The crew had tackled the upstairs
first, so she would have a place to live while the work on the
shop downstairs was completed. Then the problems started.
There had been a water leak in one of the bathrooms,
missing materials, incorrect orders, a small electrical fire.
Now it seemed almost every day something unexpected

happened. And they all cost extra time and money. But it was more than the construction delays.

The letters began showing up around the same time. At first, she thought it was some juvenile prank, a white sheet of paper with cut-out letters from a magazine saying, "I know what you did." But one after another, they had become more specific. Someone knew about her time in California over a decade ago. The last letter had come yesterday. "You didn't pay then, so you have to pay now. Everyone will know. Soon!" For the hundredth time, Charlie wondered if she had made a mistake. The minute she had stopped running, her past had caught up with her. She should have just sold this money pit and gone back on the road. Some people were not meant to have roots.

The click-clacking of little paws broke her train of thought. Mr. Bear was finished with his breakfast and was ready to play. He had a stuffed duck in his mouth. He presented it to Charlie only to turn and run under the coffee table when she reached for it, his little rump in the air, tail wagging as they played keep away for a few minutes. She laughed as he repeated the ritual over and over. She finally sat down on the oversized yellow couch. Mr. Bear jumped up beside her, placing the duck and his head on her lap. It was ironic, but he had been the deciding factor for her decision to stay in Holiday Cove.

It had rained the day of her grandmother's funeral, but half the town had come to pay their respects to Betty Ann. She had touched so many lives, and Charlie was consoled by their stories of love and generosity. Many had asked if she would be staying. Charlie knew it was what her grandmother wanted. She had said so in her letter. She had left her the house, its contents, and enough money for the renovations with a little left over to help Charlie start a new life. But Charlie had spent almost all of her adult life traveling the country. She didn't think she was the "settling down in one place" type of girl. The day had drained her of all her energy, but when she returned to the house from the graveside service, she found a soaking wet surprise on her doorstep. The little dog was half-starved and covered with mud-matted fur. She took the shivering pup inside with her, gave him some leftover roasted chicken and water, dried him off the best she could, and called the vet for an appointment the next day. She didn't intend to keep him. But he had decided he was keeping her. He followed her everywhere. When she sat down, he jumped in her lap and fell asleep.

At the vet's office, he was checked out and given his shots. The doc's best guess at his heritage was that the little pooch was a Shih Tzu mix. After the vet visit, she took him to the groomer and got him a proper bath and a haircut along with the cutest little argyle bow tie. He looked like a sweet, salt and pepper bear cub, hence his name, Mr. Bear. Charlie had never had to take care of anyone or anything but herself. But maybe it was time to try the domestic life. If she hated it, she could always sell the house and go back to traveling the country.

Now here she was six months later and still didn't know if she'd made the right choice. As soon as the downstairs was done, she could begin filling it with all of the treasures she had found over the last decade traveling the country as a picker. She had a panel truck that pulled an old, turquoise, and cream camper. Every now and then she would set up at a flea market or swap meet with whatever clothing, furniture, or knick-knacks she had on hand, but most of the time, she conducted her business online. The Vintage Gypsy website hadn't made her rich, but it met her simple needs with a little left over every month. Now she would have a storefront to go with the website if she could get Brett crew to quit making mistakes.

She stretched her arms and tried to motivate herself to leave the peace of the sunroom. Mr. Bear needed a walk, and then she needed to visit the storage unit, which was temporarily housing all of the stock for the store. As she stood up, she noticed a movement at the side of the house. One of the construction workers was headed towards a pallet of newly delivered tile for the downstairs kitchen. She watched as the worker carefully peeled back the plastic wrap. Looking around to make sure no one was watching; he took a few boxes from the stack. Charlie was horrified as he slid a few tiles from each box and pounded them with a hammer. Then he put the broken pieces back into the box. Charlie was furious. She ran downstairs and out the back door yelling to one of the workers to find Brett. As she reached the skid of tile, she caught the culprit red-handed as he was about to smash another piece of tile.

"Stop that!" Charlie shouted.

The boy looked up at Charlie in surprise.

"I--I---I'm sorry, Ms. Flynn," he stammered. "I'm afraid these boxes of tile were damaged on delivery."

"You're a liar! I saw you smash them with your hammer from upstairs."

The boy's expression changed in an instant. Gone was the apologetic, doe-eyed look of innocence. It was replaced with a steely-eyed stare from his cold blue eyes.

By this time, Brett and some of the other workers stood behind Charlie.

"Kevin, you better start explaining yourself right now," Brett said.

The boy took off his hat, his wet, blonde hair sticking to his forehead, and wiped his sweaty arm across his face. Charlie thought he couldn't be much older than twenty. She noticed patches of acne across his forehead and along his jawline. Sparse patches of hair across his chin showed a pitiful attempt at growing a beard.

Kevin pointed at Charlie. "She's crazy! Those tiles came in broken like that! I didn't do nothin' to 'em!"

Brett walked over to the pallet of tile and inspected the damaged boxes. He picked up the hammer Kevin had dropped on the ground and placed it on top of the skid.

"I don't believe you. Are you responsible for all the other stuff that's been going wrong too?" Brett crossed his arms and waited for a response.

Kevin spat on the ground. "I ain't admittin' to nothin', and it's my words against hers."

Brett's shrugged. "Fine, if that's the way you want to play this. You're fired. I'll be using your last paycheck to cover the damages."

Kevin's face turned red. "You can't do that! You can't prove I did anything!"

"Ms. Flynn caught you red-handed. That's enough for me," Brett said.

Kevin sneered at Charlie and then looked at Brett. "Better be careful who you believe, boss man. Not everybody is as innocent as they look." He spat on the ground once more and walked toward the road. Soon an old Ford truck peeled out of the drive.

"Why would he do this?" Charlie asked.

Brett let out a deep breath and scratched his head. "I don't know. This was the first job I had him on. He came to me around Christmas time begging for work. I told him we would be starting this project in January if he could hold off. Showed up that first day, and I've never had a problem out of him."

"You just never can tell about some people," Charlie sighed. "On the bright side, maybe this means no more setbacks."

Brett nodded. "I can assure you that there will be no more setbacks. If you'll excuse me, Ms. Flynn, I have a schedule to keep."

Two

rett kept his promise. The renovations were done on time, and the Vintage Gypsy was ready for its Grand Opening. Although the festivities for the Fourth wouldn't start until the following Friday, Charlie wanted the extra time to create a buzz about the store. She and Mr. Bear stood out on the front veranda admiring the transformation.

Charlie had her old camper detailed and placed it in the front yard. The turquoise stripe had been painted the same bubblegum pink as the house and the words Vintage Gypsy were painted in the same shade above the stripe. Inside the camper, employees prepared the pink snow cones, cotton candy, and pink lemonade they would be handing out through the day. A few white picnic tables placed around the giant willow tree near the camper gave guests a place to sit while they enjoyed their treats.

Pink and white balloons were tied along the white railing of the veranda, as well as the enormous Grand Opening sign by the sidewalk.

But inside was where Charlie's dream really came true. When customers entered, they would be met by the grandest staircase since Gone with the Wind. The stairs and banisters were made of white marble with veins of silver and grey. Two topiaries with pink, blooming flowers stood on each side, and a hand-made, scrolled, wrought iron gate prevented anyone from going upstairs. In front of the staircase was a large mahogany counter with the same marble as the staircase for the countertop. Two computers for checkout were at each end. Above the counter was a glamorous chandelier of pink and silver crystals. It radiated a soft blush light over the entrance. Two silver armchairs in crushed velvet and a couple of satin-covered pink benches polished off the opulent space.

To the left of the entrance was the converted library. Charlie had been able to restore the wall of floor to ceiling bookshelves. They were now filled with a collection of books that would rival most libraries. Rare collectible books locked up in antique glass cases stood in front of the shelves. The room was spacious and held many of Charlie's unique finds like an old suit of armor, a baccarat table, several Tiffany lamps, and two original Stickley chairs. Vintage board games lined the two shelves that flanked the fireplace. Charlie had even set up a cozy nook in front of the fireplace where customers could read or play a board game. The library flowed into a hallway leading to what was once a formal parlor.

It had been transformed into a fashionista's dream. Charlie had curated a collection that had everything from vintage rock band t-shirts, old Levi's, and saddle shoes to genuine Victorian top hats, authentic poodle skirts, and pristine Bob Mackie gowns. Two pink mid-century modern couches on a white shag rug were centered in the middle of the room. Issues of Glamour, Vogue, and Vanity Fair from almost every decade in circulation were piled on a sleek glass coffee table. Full-length mirrors stood in every corner, and circular marble display cases showed off retro Gucci and Fendi bags, Prada shoes, and Louis Vuitton luggage. Clear display cases were lined with jewelry to fit any taste and budget from a pair of feather earrings to a classic Pave broach. At the back of the room were two luxuriously designed dressing rooms with crystal chandeliers and golden damask benches and chairs.

A small hallway led from the clothing area to a sitting room on the enclosed sun porch. A long floral couch faced the manicured lawn. A couple of wicker chairs and a cafe table sat beside an old-fashioned drink cart holding baskets filled with snacks. A large metal tub filled with ice stood in the corner filled with mini bottles of soda and water.

A longer hallway led to the private part of the first floor where Charlie's office was. The downstairs kitchen and a small dining area were beside the office. A back staircase to Charlie's apartment and an additional exit were off the other side of the kitchen.

To the right of the entrance was where most of the renovations had taken place. All the walls were taken out to make one grand room. Shelves and display cases were filled with items from all over the country. There were old signs, movie posters, furniture, knick-knacks, old toys, a jukebox, Hummel figurines, anything a collector could ask for.

Charlie was satisfied after her walk around the grounds and the interior that everything was in place and ready for the day.

"We better start getting ready, Mr. Bear. We can't be late to our own party."

Mr. Bear barked in agreement, and the pair headed upstairs.

Charlie had one weakness. Clothes. She had converted one of the smaller bedrooms into her closet. Vintage clothes, shoes, and purses lined the walls. Mr. Bear waited patiently as Charlie paced the floor. She wanted to wear something festive and was having trouble finding the right outfit. A flash of yellow caught her eye. She grabbed the hanger and tried it on. She was pleased as she looked at herself in the mirror. The Halston jumpsuit fit her perfectly. She loved the wide legs and cinched belt. The blouse fit loosely over her chest and arms. It accentuated her curves without clinging to them, and the length was just right. At 5'9, sometimes things didn't hang right on her frame. But the jumpsuit was perfect. She wished she had time to straighten her curly red locks to complete the seventies vibe, but that would take too much time. Instead, she grabbed a psychedelic Pucci scarf and used it as a headband. She rummaged through her jewelry armoire and pulled out a stack of brightly colored acrylic bangles, a necklace with a large tangerine pendant, and a pair of gold hoop earrings. She slipped on some gold sandals before she sat down at the make-up table. She wrinkled her nose at her reflection. She'd be thirty-five in a few months but could still pass for her late twenties. She'd always taken care of her skin. Since she was pale, her skin burned easily, so she always used sunscreen. Sometimes she would find a few silver streaks of hair hiding amongst her fiery curls, but she didn't really care. She placed a shimmery shade of taupe across her eyelid. The shimmer brought out the golden flecks of her hazel eyes. She applied a little eyeliner, mascara, and some apricot gloss to her lips, then she was ready to go. She walked to a small dresser and opened the drawer.

"Mr. Bear, what would you like to wear today?"

Charlie browsed through the selection of bowties and kerchiefs. She found a bowtie that was similar to her headband with bold geometric patterns of yellow, orange, and turquoise. She placed it around his neck, and he barked in approval.

She locked the apartment up and walked back downstairs just as her assistant walked through the front door.

Susan Oakes was Charlie's right hand. Although she was younger than Charlie by more than a decade, she had an old soul. Charlie hadn't been thrilled about needing an assistant. She was used to working alone and didn't want to take the time to teach someone the ropes. But she knew that she wouldn't be able to keep up the online business, the storefront, and the picking by herself. She had probably interviewed twenty people before Susan had come along. Charlie had snatched her away from her hostess gig at the Chick-N-Hen, the local diner where Charlie had conducted her interviews. She had watched the young girl handle the crowded restaurant like a pro. Susan stayed focused and calm even at the busiest rush hours, treated the customers with kindness and respect, and always had a smile on her freckled face. She reminded Charlie of Popeye's girlfriend, Olive Oyl because she was tall and thin and kept her ebony hair in a tight bun on top of her head. Charlie had never seen her wear anything but the color black. But she had been impressed when Susan had been able to stop a fight between two rather large farm boys. She had forced her way between them, hands on hips, and warned them any attempt to continue acting like juveniles would result in a boot in their backsides and a permanent ban from the diner. The boys backed off. Whether it was because they didn't want to get their butts kicked by a ninety-pound girl or banned from the place that sold the best fried chicken in three states didn't matter to Charlie. She liked the girl's style. After the lunch rush, she had introduced herself to Susan and offered her a job right on the spot. Susan was thrilled. She had taken classes in administration at the local community college and had gotten a degree but had trouble finding work in the field. Hiring Susan had been one of the best decisions Charlie had ever made. She had even taken her on a couple of picking runs and was impressed with her eye for things that would sell.

"Hello, Mr. Bear!" Susan cooed. "I brought you a present."

Mr. Bear ran to Susan and looked at her expectantly. She reached into the pocket of her black dress and offered him a bacon treat. He grabbed it from her hand and was off to the dog bed they put behind the counter for him.

"That will keep him busy for all of ten seconds," Charlie laughed.

Susan smiled. "Then we better get started while he's distracted."

They walked towards Charlie's office as she went over the day's agenda with Susan.

"The others should be here in a few minutes. We need at least two people in the camper, three on the floor in here, and two at checkout. You and I will pitch in where we are needed."

Susan nodded and brought out her iPad to assign everyone to a station, talking as she typed.

"I think we'll be busy. People are going to come just to see what you've done to the house."

They did one last walk around, and Charlie made a few changes here and there. "I don't care why they come, just as long as they don't walk out empty-handed."

Susan was right. They were busy. Curiosity about Charlie and the renovated mansion brought them in, but they stayed and shopped. Charlie had not seen anyone leave without purchasing a little something. Before she knew it, her stomach was growling that it was way past lunchtime. She knew her employees had worked hard too and needed a break, so she called in a lunch order to the Chick-N-Hen and requested it to be delivered.

The crowds just kept coming. Charlie was busy helping a sweet older woman in the great room pick out a Civil War era knife for her husband, so she didn't see Kevin Wilson making a beeline towards her.

"Happy Grand Opening to the queen!" Kevin bowed. He stood on wobbly legs and was slurring his speech.

Charlie plastered on a smile. She'd dealt with drunks before and knew she needed to handle the situation quickly before it got out of hand. She spotted Susan following him into the room.

"Kevin, why don't you go to the kitchen with Susan? She'll get you a cup of hot coffee."

"I don't want coffee. I came to shop," he sneered.

He picked up a ceramic teapot from a nearby shelf.

"A hundred dollars? Is it made of gold?"

He laughed to himself as he tried to place the teapot back on the shelf. But it came crashing to the ground, shards of glazed ceramic flying everywhere.

"Oops! Don't worry your highness, I'll pay for that. Oh, wait! I can't pay for that because you got me fired." He pointed a finger at Charlie.

She could feel the heat on her cheeks.

"You got yourself fired, Kevin. But this isn't the time or place to talk about it. Don't worry about the teapot; just let Susan help you to the kitchen."

By now, everyone was watching the interaction between the two. Charlie noticed the girl from the diner had brought lunch and was standing there by the knife case, a look of bewilderment on her face. Charlie needed to diffuse the situation. She motioned for Susan to approach Kevin, but he pushed past her and closed in on Charlie. Everyone in the room stopped to watch the train wreck in front of them.

He leaned in close enough to Charlie where she could smell the acrid booze on his breath.

"You have all this, but I could bring your world crumbling down around you like that!" He tried to snap his fingers. "Like that!" He tried again. He giggled to himself. Then looked at Charlie with that piercing stare.

"What would all these decent people do if they knew the truth about you? You would lose everything, wouldn't you? That'd knock you off that high horse you've been ridin' around on."

Kevin grabbed her arm and tried to pull Charlie towards him. Charlie panicked and with her free hand, took the knife she had been showing her customer and placed the tip underneath his chin.

"You let go of me right now. Leave and never come back here, or I will call the police, and have you buried under the jail. Do you understand me?"

Kevin giggled again as he wiped a drop of blood from his chin.

"Sure, I'll leave. But this ain't over. The truth always comes out, and you don't have anywhere left to run."

Kevin pushed the crowd away and staggered out the door.

Charlie watched him go and a pit formed in her stomach. She knew she had found her pen pal and was going to have a long talk with him as soon as he sobered up.

Three

Charlie noticed the silence and that everyone was looking at her. She somehow managed a weak smile and spoke to her guests.

"Well, folks, things are not going to be boring here at The Vintage Gypsy."

After a few awkward moments, people started going back to whatever they were doing before. Charlie couldn't find the woman she had been helping, but she saw the delivery girl with the lunch order, so she laid the knife back in the display case and motioned for the girl to follow her into the kitchen. She and Susan gave the other employees a few minutes for a break.

It was almost closing time by the time everyone finished eating, so Charlie and Susan waited for the last customers to leave before heading to the kitchen. Susan heated up the cold chicken while Charlie poured Mr. Bear a bowl of kibble. Susan brought the plates of food to the table, and they both began to eat, too exhausted to speak. They were almost finished eating when they heard someone knock on the back door. Charlie went to answer it, and a few seconds later reappeared back in the kitchen with her best friend, Nan Holiday. Nan sat down and placed a box of freshly baked cupcakes on the table.

"I feel like a loser for missing your big day," she said. "The store was packed all day, and I had two girls out sick."

Charlie waved her off her apology as she opened the cupcake box. Nan ran one of the most popular boutiques in town and was always busy.

"All is forgiven when you bring something from Hal's. Blueberry Lemonade! My favorite!" Charlie took a big bite out of one of the cupcakes while she started a fresh pot of coffee.

"You did miss the action though," Susan said.

Charlie tried to shake her head, but it was too late. Nan was going to overreact. She had appointed herself Charlie's protector years ago on a park playground. A couple of local girls were making fun of Charlie's hair, and little pint-sized Nan was not having it. She pushed one of the girls down to the dirt and threatened the other girl with a black eye. Charlie's tormentors didn't hang around to see if Nan would make good on her threat. From then on, the girls were inseparable. When Charlie came to spend summers with her grandmother, Nan was always there. As they grew older, Charlie realized why Nan had to be so tough. It wasn't easy growing up poor in an affluent town like Holiday Cove, but Nan refused to let anyone treat her differently because she didn't wear the right clothes or live in a fancy neighborhood. Even as a kid, Nan always took the side of the underdog. She knew a person's character had nothing to do with a bank account. Yes, Nan was a little bossy, but Charlie hadn't minded. She admired Nan's no-nonsense view of the world.

Now they were adults, and she was no less bossy and worried more than she should about Charlie's well-being. Charlie didn't want Nan prying into this, and she definitely didn't want her husband, Detective Lance Holiday nosing around.

"What happened?" Nan demanded to know. She got up and walked over to Charlie. She folded her arms and leaned against the counter. There was a lot of attitude in such a small frame. Nan was barely 5'4 but always wore heels that made her almost as tall as Charlie and always looked like she'd stepped out of a fashion magazine. Her blonde hair cascaded in waves over shoulders. The turquoise tunic she was wearing brought out the blue of her eyes, which at this minute were boring a hole through Charlie. She tapped her perfectly pedicured toe and waited for Charlie to fill her in on the day's events.

Charlie sighed. The cat was out of the bag now.

"Go sit back down, and I'll tell you over a cup of coffee."

Nan made a face but obliged. Once they were all sitting back down at the table, Charlie told her story.

"I had a run-in with the guy that was sabotaging the construction site."

She tried to downplay the details as she told Nan what had happened, but she wasn't buying it.

"I'm calling Lance like you should have done when that boy started threatening you!"

"Oh, she held her own," Susan said. "She pulled a knife on him."

Charlie rolled her eyes. "Thanks, friend." She turned to Nan.

"It was instinct," she shrugged. "All those self-defense classes just kicked in."

Nan put her hand on her hip. "I guess I missed Knife-Wielding 101 in my class."

Susan was about to say something else when Charlie kicked her underneath the table. She got the message and kept her mouth shut.

"Nan, it wasn't a big deal. He was drunk and blames me for getting fired."

"Why was he doing those things to you in the first place?" Nan asked.

Charlie shook her head. "I think he's just some messed up kid, and for whatever reason, he was trying to make Brett look bad. I just got caught in the cross-fire."

"Brett's a good man with a good reputation. It would take more than that to affect his business," Susan said.

Charlie noticed the tone change in Susan's voice. There was a softness to it when she talked about Brett.

"But what I don't understand is what secret he was talking about. It seems he's trying to ruin you, not Brett," Susan continued.

Both women stared at Charlie, waiting for an answer.

"I have no idea! Maybe I just attract crazy. But I have nothing to hide, no secrets," Charlie lied.

"He could have you confused with someone else," Nan pursed her lips.

"That or he's just a troublemaker. Some people derive pleasure from stirring things up. It's probably as simple as that." Charlie got up to get another cup of coffee, signaling she was done with the subject.

However, Nan wasn't ready to let Charlie off the hook.

"Charlie, this is something you shouldn't be so flippant about. This guy could be dangerous. You live here alone. What if he shows up again without an audience?"

"Mr. Bear is better than any alarm system. If it moves, he barks. Plus, I have one of the best non-canine alarm systems on the market. I'm not worried."

Nan sighed. She knew she was fighting a losing battle. But she'd tell Lance anyway. Maybe he could send an officer to patrol the area for the night. What Charlie didn't know wouldn't hurt her.

After Nan and Susan left, Charlie locked the door and cleaned up the kitchen. She did a final walk through the downstairs and turned off all the lights. She knew she wouldn't be able to sleep that night if she didn't find out what Kevin knew. She took Mr. Bear upstairs and put him in his kennel with his favorite toy. He was not happy about being left behind, and he barked in protest as Charlie left the apartment, her Glock 19 secure in her purse.

Four

Charlie woke up the next morning with Mr. Bear using her toes as a chew toy. She squealed and put her feet back under the blanket. Now she remembered why she didn't make a habit of letting him sleep in the bed with her. The dog was worse than an alarm clock. Mr. Bear bounded off the bed and grabbed one of his toys from the floor before hopping back up to snuggle beside her. She opened one eye to see him with a stuffed carrot in his mouth. She grabbed the toy and threw it off the bed. He jumped from the bed, sliding across the hardwood floors. Pleased with his retrieval, he brought the toy back to Charlie. They played a few more rounds of fetch before she got out of bed. Last night had been a wasted effort. She'd gotten Kevin's address from Brett. Once she got there, she had second thoughts about getting out of the truck. The battered single wide was in the middle of nowhere, and she couldn't tell if anyone was home. There were no vehicles in the driveway, but she saw the lights of the TV through one of the windows. She had almost made it to the porch when she heard a deep growl. She turned to see a dog the size of a small pony coming at her. She ran back towards the truck but tripped over a limb. The dog kept coming. In the dark, she couldn't see the chain that held him back. He stopped just short of her feet, straining at his chain, jaws snapping in the air. Charlie crawled on her hands and feet, trying to escape the ferocious fangs. Some of the contents of her purse spilled out onto the ground. She quickly gathered her things up, managed to stand on shaky legs, and made a dash to the truck, never bothering to look back. On the way home, she got lost and didn't get in until after two that morning. With only three hours of sleep, she would need extra caffeine to make it through the day. She put on her robe and a pot of coffee and went downstairs to let Mr. Bear out for his morning patrol of the grounds. She watched as he pranced around the perimeter of the yard, making sure everything was in place. Once satisfied that his domain was intact, he proceeded to fertilize the flowerbed before joining Charlie on the veranda.

"You're a good boy! Let's go get some breakfast!"

Mr. Bear immediately took off towards the stairs. Charlie swore that dog understood every word she said.

She sipped her coffee and nibbled on a leftover cupcake while she watched the sunrise. She had never felt like she belonged anywhere until the day she decided to make Holiday Cove her home. The only unhappy memory she had here was of her grandmother's death, and that was almost overshadowed by all the good memories Betty Ann had created for her. If Kevin made good on his threat to expose Charlie's secret, all that happiness would be gone. Of course, she really didn't believe she deserved happiness anyway even though these last few months had been pleasant. She had made friends, created a life for herself. She wasn't ready to let that go yet. She would deal with Kevin as soon as she could find him. But until then she had a job to do. She finished her breakfast and prepared for her day.

She didn't expect as big of a crowd since it felt like most of the town had come out yesterday, but she was still hoping for some tourist traffic. She put on a long blue and white polka-dotted button up with cuffed jeans and mint condition saddle shoes. She had no desire to deal with her crazy curls, so she piled them on top of her head in a messy bun and tied a white scarf around them. She found a matching polka dot tie for Mr. Bear, and they were off to work. Charlie had just finished turning on the lights when Susan walked in. She didn't look like she had slept well either.

"I have some coffee brewing," Charlie said. "It looks like you could use some."

Susan nodded and mumbled something unintelligible as she walked toward the kitchen. Today's black ensemble seemed to match her mood. Charlie followed her into the kitchen for a second cup of coffee.

Mr. Bear was already there, contently chewing on the new toy Susan had brought him.

"I think he may be the most spoiled dog in Holiday Cove," Charlie said.

"Probably," Susan agreed.

"Do you want to talk about what's got you down this morning?" Charlie asked.

"Charlie, Kevin Wilson was found murdered this morning. Someone shot him. Brett called me after Lance stopped by to ask him some questions. He said you called him last night asking for Kevin's address."

"I did. I was going to talk to him."

"Did you go out there last night?"

"No. It was too late, and I'm not dumb enough to go out there alone." Charlie hated lying, but she couldn't admit to being there now that Kevin was dead. How close had she come to being there at the same time as his killer?

"Thank goodness. I'd guess Lance will be coming around here, wanting to talk to you next."

As if on cue, there was a knock on the back door and Charlie went to answer it. Lance followed her into the kitchen.

"I understand you've had a busy morning," Charlie said. "Pull up a seat, and I'll pour you a cup of coffee."

Lance fiddled with the old cowboy hat he was holding. "This isn't a social visit, Charlie."

"I know. Sit down anyway. Just because we have to talk business doesn't mean we can't be civil."

Susan excused herself and took Mr. Bear with her, leaving Lance and Charlie to speak alone. Lance was a direct descendant of Vic Holiday. Both his mother and father had been mayor of Holiday Cove at one time and everyone expected Lance would run in the next election. He and Nan had been high school sweethearts. He was the All-American quarterback, and she was the head cheerleader. They'd gotten married sometime after college, but had never had children; instead, they concentrated on their careers and community. Charlie didn't know Lance as well as she did Nan. When Charlie had come to live with Betty Ann her senior year in high school after her parents had died, Nan and Lance were in a rocky patch, so she didn't see much of him. But he hadn't seemed to change much. He still had most of his thick black hair and boyish charm. He'd always worn Levi's and cowboy boots with a nice button-up shirt, although now, the buttons strained ever so slightly around his mid-section. Some crow's feet danced around his dark brown eyes, and shards of grey had found their way into his mustache and beard. But he still gave some of the young bucks a run for their money during the annual community football game in November. He laid his Stetson on the table and sat down across from Charlie.

"So, you heard about Kevin?" Lance asked.

Charlie nodded.

"What do you reckon this fella had against you?"

Charlie took a sip of coffee. "It's like I told Nan last night. I don't think it was personal. I think he was just one of those people that liked stirring up trouble, and he thought he found an easy target in me."

"I guess he had second thoughts about that when you pulled a knife on him," Lance tried to hide a smile.

Charlie sighed. Nan had a big mouth. "Listen, he grabbed my arm, and I felt threatened. In hindsight, I could have handled it better, I guess."

"What I want to know is why you didn't you call me?"

"He already blamed me for getting him fired," Charlie replied. "I didn't want him blaming me for getting thrown into jail too. He was just a dumb kid that had too much to drink."

Lance took out his notebook. "You asked Brett for his address. Did you go out there?"

"No." Charlie was getting good at lying. "After I thought about it, I knew it was a bad idea."

"Where were you early this mornin', around two?" Lance asked.

"Here. Alone. I went to bed early. We'd had a busy day."

"You don't happen to have a gun, do you?"

Charlie hesitated. "Not personally. I do have some antique firearms in the store, though." She looked at Lance and knew he didn't believe her.

He took one last sip of his coffee, stood up, and grabbed his hat.

"Lots of people saw y'all go at it yesterday. I have to follow this investigation wherever it leads, including your front door. But, as a friend, I'd say it might not be a bad idea for you to give Andy a call."

"That's good advice, I will." It must be bad if Lance wanted her to call a lawyer.

Five

As soon as Lance left, Charlie ran upstairs. Her gun was missing! It must have fallen out of her purse at Kevin's. She had obtained it illegally years ago for her safety. The only way it could be identified as hers was if they ran a fingerprint test. As soon as she left Andy's, she'd sneak back up to Kevin's to see if she could find it before someone else did.

Andy Brock was the only other friend that Charlie kept in touch with from her childhood in Holiday Cove. His mother had been Betty Ann's caregiver after her grandfather had passed away. Betty Ann had a small stroke that had left her unable to do all the things she was used to. The big house was too much for her to take care of, but it had been in the Flynn family since Holiday Cove was first settled.

Charlie knew her grandmother had hung on to it for her. Sheila Brock came over two or three times a week to help clean, do some laundry, and make a few meals. She was one of the best cooks in the county. And she always brought fresh eggs and churned butter from the Brock farm.

Charlie and Andy would play under the Willow tree while Sheila tended to her work. Some days they would play nicely. Other days not so much. Once Andy had accused Charlie of saying a curse word. Betty Ann had washed Charlie's mouth out with soap. Charlie had retaliated by pushing Andy out of the Willow tree. She had never been so scared in her life when he wouldn't stop crying. The fall had broken his arm. She waited for her punishment, but it never came. Andy had kept her secret.

Andy still lived on the Brock farm, but he had gotten his law degree from the University of Tennessee. He shared his time between the farm and a small law office on Main Street. He was undoubtedly Holiday Cove's most eligible bachelor. His hair had started turning grey during high school. Now his silver hair and icy blue eyes gave him a distinguished look. Charlie had never been much of a fan of facial hair, but even she had to admit Andy's neatly trimmed, salt and pepper beard suited him. He always wore overalls or jeans on the farm and a suit with a vest when he practiced law. Try as they might, the matchmakers of the tiny town had not been able to persuade Andy to leave the single life. The only companion he needed was his Golden Retriever, Gus. Andy had handled Betty Ann's estate for her when she passed, along with all of Charlie's business's legal needs. The gossip mill was disappointed when no fireworks sparked between the two friends. Somehow the broken could always spot one of their own, and Charlie knew Andy was a broken man.

It was a lovely day, so she'd just walk the two blocks to Andy's office. She grabbed Mr. Bear's leash and said the magic words.

"Let's go for a walk."

The happy pup bounded towards her, tail wagging, ready to go. Andy's office was dog-friendly since he rarely went anywhere without Gus. His office was in an old brick storefront between Ben Howard's Barbershop and Stan White's hardware store. You could smell the testosterone from the street. Some of the Cove's finest senior citizens sat out on a bench in front of the barbershop with cups of coffee in their hands watching the world go by. Charlie spotted Andy's baby blue 1940's Ford truck in front of his office. She waved to the senior crew as she walked by. Mr. Bear and Gus greeted each other with friendly barks as Andy stepped into the lobby.

"Hey, Charlie! Did we have an appointment this morning?"

Charlie shook her head. "No. I was hoping you'd be here and have a few minutes to spare for me."

"Sure, I've always got time for you, Moll. I don't have to be in court for an hour. Come on back."

Charlie cringed at her nickname. Andy had grown up watching old black and white gangster movies with his dad and could quote almost every line from anything with James Cagney in it. After Charlie had pushed him out of the tree, he had started calling her Moll, the word for a female gangster. He said it was because she was a "dame that knew how to even the score." Thankfully, he had grown out of his gangster phase and antiquated names for women. But he had not given up her nickname.

She followed him down the hall to his private office. There was nothing fancy about the space. It was simple, just like him. There were no plants, no pictures, no personal mementos. The only furnishings were an oak desk, a leather chair, two armchairs, and a bookcase filled only with law books. A lonely framed law degree hung on the wall behind his desk.

"Where's Ms. Hayes?" Charlie asked as they sat down.

"Visiting her sister in Chattanooga for the week. I feel like I'm missing my right arm."

Marcy Hayes was Andy's secretary. She doted on him since the death of his mother and kept his office running like a well-oiled machine. She was a no-nonsense, get-to-the-point kind of person, but she had a soft spot for Andy.

Charlie didn't know how to begin. She knew she had to be careful, so she watched her words.

"Lance recommended I come to see you. There was an altercation at the shop yesterday. A miserable young man that blamed me for losing his job and made some threats. I responded somewhat aggressively. The man ended up murdered last night."

Andy raised an eyebrow. "Somewhat aggressively? Just how gangster did you get?"

Charlie didn't want to tell him. "I pulled a knife on him and threatened to bury him under the jail."

"You've got to be kidding me! You can't just go around pulling knives on people, even if they deserve it. Is Lance considering you a suspect?" Andy sounded worried.

"Not yet. I think this morning's visit was the last concession from him I'm going to get. A room full of people saw what happened yesterday. I think he doesn't want to be accused of favoritism. If he can't find another viable suspect, he will question me, and said so in no uncertain terms."

"Charlie, I handle wills and estates, maybe the occasional business start-up like yours. I don't practice criminal law. Why don't you go to talk to Dottie Buchannon? She does criminal work."

"I'm not a criminal, yet. Plus, I don't know her. I know you, Andy. I just want you there if I have to be questioned."

Andy fidgeted with his cufflinks. "Is there anything else I should know?"

"No." Charlie hated to keep lying.

"I'm already on retainer for your business account. I'll whip up a personal contract after I get back from court. I'll bring it by for you to sign when I'm finished."

"Thank you, Andy." She stood to leave.

They walked to the front door together to find the dogs playing tug of war with one of Gus's toys. Charlie put Mr. Bear's leash on and tried to ignore Andy's gaze. He didn't believe her, but she'd have to worry about that later.

Six

Charlie was surprised by the crowd at the Vintage Gypsy when she returned from Andy's. Though it wasn't as much as the previous day, it was still more than she anticipated. Two of the staff were swamped at the cash registers and small crowds of people milled around the store. Mr. Bear made his way to his bed behind the counter, stopping only to enjoy the occasional pat or ear rub. Charlie found Susan helping a young girl decide between a Versace leather jacket or a pair of Prada pumps. Charlie smiled at the customer.

"You should get both. The pumps pair perfectly with the jacket. I'll take twenty-five percent off, and you'll have the perfect outfit!"

The girl thought for a moment, and a big grin appeared on her face. Charlie wrote a ticket for her to take to check out.

"Someone's in a generous mood," Susan teased.

"Why make them choose if they don't have to?" Charlie winked. "Listen, I know it's busy, but I need you to take care of things here for the rest of the day. I have some things I need to do."

Susan eyed her suspiciously. "Don't do anything that will get you into trouble."

"Trouble has already found me. Buy lunch for everyone from petty cash, and if Mr. Bear is too much to handle just put him back in his kennel upstairs."

"Anything else?" Susan asked.

"Andy Brock's supposed to bring by some papers for me to sign," Charlie replied. "If I'm not back by then just leave them in the office and tell him I'll have them on his desk first thing in the morning."

Charlie left out of the back entrance to the detached garage behind the big house. Her love for all things retro didn't extend to cars. Although she was an admirer of vintage automobiles, she loved the modern technology of newer models. And since she always had an eye out for her next big purchase, she needed a vehicle that had plenty of room. When she decided to stay in Holiday Cove, she had purchased a brand new Ford F-150 in cherry red. It was her baby and had more than enough room to handle all of Charlie's finds for the store.

Kevin's address was still on her GPS from the night before. She'd have to remember to delete it after she was done. The trailer was out in the county down a long curvy

road. Charlie drove by the driveway, cordoned off with
yellow police tape. There was a walking trail to an old spring
just a little further up from Kevin's drive. She followed the
dirt road and parked her truck off to the side. She got out
an old pair of gloves from the glove box and put them in
her back pocket. She found an old trucker's hat she had
forgotten about behind the seat and tucked her mass of red
curls underneath it. She walked back to Kevin's, staying
close to the road but in the woods so she wouldn't be
noticed. She stayed out of sight as she trudged up the long
driveway. She kept an eye out for the gun and the big angry
dog. In the light of day, she could see the doghouse at the
side of the trailer. Both the chain and the dog were gone.
Charlie crawled along the grass on her hands and knees
looking for the gun. Her heart sank. It wasn't there. She
looked towards the road to make sure nobody was coming.

She needed to get inside that trailer. If Kevin was the
one sending her the letters, she had to find the evidence and
destroy it. She walked to the back door to see if she could
find a way in. A rickety set of stairs led to the door. No
yellow tape here. Maybe they had forgotten to lock the
door. She turned the knob, but no such luck. Charlie looked
around. A row of three windows lined the backside of the
trailer. If her luck changed, one of them could have been
left unlocked. She found a bucket sturdy enough to stand
on and hit the jackpot on the first window she tried. It was
a squeeze, but she made it through. The smell of stale beer
and old blood assaulted her senses. She had come through

the laundry room that was to the right of the kitchen. The floor was spongy under her feet. A dining table stood in the center, and dark, sticky blood stains thickened beneath it. Charlie fought back the urge to gag. She stepped across the blood and walked into the living room. The bedrooms were down the hall, and that's where she'd start. She had given herself a time limit of fifteen minutes. Any more than that and she'd risk being caught. The bedroom was disgusting.

Dirty socks and underwear littered the floor. A stained mattress and busted dresser were the only furnishings. Charlie quickly lifted the mattress and felt underneath it. It only took her a minute to rifle through the chest since it just held a few items of clothing. She opened the closet and found a small box deep in the corner of the top shelf. She took it out to inspect it closer. It was an old lock box. She rummaged through the closet again to see if she could find the key. Time was running out. The box could contain what she was looking for, but she didn't have time to try and break into it here. She did a quick once over in the bathroom and the other bedroom as well as the living room. She opened every drawer and cabinet in the kitchen and found no key. She decided she'd have to take the lockbox with her. She hoped the police hadn't noticed it. She snuck out the back door and to her truck without incident.

Once she got back to the house, she hid the lockbox among some Christmas decorations in the garage. She walked through the back door and heard voices in the kitchen. Andy and Susan were having coffee.

"Oh, no!" Susan shouted. "What happened to your shoes?"

Charlie looked down at her feet. Her beautiful saddle shoes were ruined from walking in the woods. Why hadn't she thought to change them before traipsing in the woods?

"I was running errands and passed by a junk sale. I got to digging around in the barn and must have gotten them dirty there."

Charlie was going to have to start writing down all of her lies so she could keep up with them.

"I brought your papers by, if you want to take a look and sign them, we can be official today," Andy said.

Susan stood up. "I'll let y'all get to business. I need to check on the store, anyway."

Andy brought the paperwork out while Charlie poured herself a cup of coffee.

"That's the second time you've lied today. Do you want to tell me what's going on or do I continue to play dumb lawyer?"

Charlie didn't turn around. "If you're uncomfortable with being my lawyer, I can find someone else."

Andy rose from the chair and stood beside her.

"Moll, I'm not some hayseed farmer with a Cracker Jack box law degree, and I'm not the boy you pushed out of a tree. I learned a long time ago, the consequences of naivety. My eyes are wide open. I don't care if you tell me the truth or not. But I won't allow you to play me for a fool."

Charlie turned to face him. She looked into those angry blue eyes and felt their penetrating gaze. "I never have and never will take you for a fool. I need to deal with this my own way. I won't lie to you anymore, but that doesn't mean I'm going to tell you everything."

Andy drew a deep breath. He caught the scent of her magnolia shampoo mingled with sweat. Her mascara had smeared under her eyes. Her blouse was wrinkled, and there was a spot of mud on her jeans. She didn't have to say anything. He knew exactly where she'd been, but he'd let her keep her secret. It wasn't like he didn't have any of his own.

"I'm your lawyer, and I'm your friend. You don't have to tell me anything you don't want to, but you can't lie to me. Deal?"

"Deal," Charlie said. "Now, where are those papers you need me to sign?

Seven

After everyone had left for the day, Charlie snuck back out to the garage and retrieved the box. She went upstairs and placed it on the kitchen table. It took her a few minutes, but she finally unlocked the box with a paperclip. Her stomach turned when she saw the contents. Kevin had not been bluffing. Somehow, he had found out about her past. Her hands shook as she read the newspaper clippings and looked at the photographs he had collected. She kept digging through the box, faces of her past haunting her. She found an envelope with her name on it. It was a letter just like the other ones. She doubted if Lance or anyone else would believe in her innocence if they found the contents of this box. She closed her eyes, willing herself not to cry. It was over now. She was probably one of Kevin's many victims. That type of life catches up with you. Someone had taken care of Charlie's problem for her, and worrying wasn't going to get her anywhere.

Mr. Bear began to whine at her feet. She'd been so engrossed in the box, she'd lost track of time, but the dog hadn't. He knew it was time for dinner. Her stomach growled, reminding her she hadn't eaten since breakfast. She didn't feel like cooking, and nothing looked appetizing to her in the fridge. Checking the time, she decided to clean up and have dinner at the Chick-N-Hen. She fed the hungry pooch first, then changed into a clean Rolling Stones t-shirt and a fresh pair of jeans. Her hair was a frizzy mess, but she tamed it back into a ponytail. She layered on a bit of lip gloss and powdered her nose. It would have to do. After putting Mr. Bear in his kennel with a biscuit and a toy, she was finally ready to leave. She slipped into a pair of Converse she had by the door and walked out into the warm night air.

She had plenty of time to get to the restaurant before it closed, so she decided to walk. It would give her some time to clear her head. The tiny restaurant was crowded as usual. Red and white gingham tablecloths draped the dining tables down the center aisle, and bright red booths lined the outer walls. A vast collection of chickens and hens crowded the plate rail that ran along the upper walls. Smells of home cooking wafted from the noisy kitchen. Almost every table was full. The hostess was about to seat Charlie when she heard her name.

"Charlie Flynn!"

Charlie looked through the crowd and saw a tiny, wrinkled hand waving in her direction. She smiled as she walked over to see Ms. Ada Hedgecoth. Ms. Ada had been her grandmother's dearest friend. Charlie felt a twinge of guilt that she had not been to see her in a few weeks. Charlie bent down and gave her a gentle hug. Although Ms. Ada was well into her eighties, she had the health and vigor of someone twenty years younger. She kept her white hair in a neat pixie cut, and every inch of her makeup was flawless. She always wore something colorful and flowing. Tonight she had on a bright red, floral kimono over an emerald-green pantsuit. Bangles adorned each arm, and large gold earrings framed her face.

"Sit with me, child. I just placed my order, and now I won't have to eat alone."

Charlie was actually thankful for the company and gladly sat down across from her new dinner companion. The server brought Charlie a menu. She recognized her from the delivery she'd made on the day Kevin had threatened her. The name tag in the shape of a chicken had "Lila" in big red letters. She looked to be around Charlie's age. There was sadness in her hazel eyes that told a story. Life had not been kind. She wore her auburn hair in a single long braid down her back. Charlie noticed a partial bruise around her upper arm that her uniform didn't cover. It looked to be in the shape of fingers. The girl caught Charlie staring and tugged on her sleeve to try to hide the bruise.

Charlie gave her an embarrassed smile. "Y'all are busy tonight."

Lila didn't return her smile. "We are. Do you know what you want, or do you need a minute?"

"I'll have the fried chicken, mashed potatoes with no gravy, fried okra, and a sweet tea, please."

Lila finished writing her order and grabbed an empty basket from the table. "I'll be back with more biscuits and your tea. Ms. Ada, do you need a refill?"

"Yes please, dear. Just whenever you have time."

Lila smiled at Ms. Ada and disappeared into the kitchen.

"Charlie, I plan on visiting your store tomorrow. My daughter and her family are coming in, and I want to bring them."

"That will be wonderful! Come towards the end of the day. I'll give you the grand tour, then we'll have dinner afterward. You can see all I've done to the upstairs."

Ms. Ada beamed. "I would love to. Your grandmother would be so proud of you and all you've done to that monstrosity of a house."

Charlie laughed. "It was an undertaking, but Grandma loved that house, and it's all I have left of her and my parents."

Charlie didn't talk much about her parents. Her mother, Carol, had been Betty Ann and Charles Flynn's only child. Charlie's mother had met her father, Roger, when they were both in college. He had been a foster child and was on his own at eighteen. He worked his way through college and met Carol in his senior year. They were married that summer. Her dad had wanted to serve both his country and others. He enrolled in seminary so that he could become a Chaplain in the military. Charlie was born on an army base in Germany. Her parents traveled the world with her dad's career. It was where Charlie's wanderlust began. Nevertheless, every summer, Charlie called the pink mansion and Holiday Cove home.

Tragically, her parents died in a car crash the summer before Charlie's senior year of high school. Charlie knew Betty Ann wanted her to attend college somewhere close to home. However, Charlie wanted out of the town that had somehow gone from a place of refuge to an albatross around her neck. She went as far away from Tennessee as she could. She enrolled in a small college in Valencia, California as an Art History major. Her dream was to travel the globe, acquiring hard to find artistic works for museums and private collectors. Now, she often wondered if she had stayed in Tennessee how different her life would be. Her dream had turned into a nightmare, and sometimes she felt like nothing more than an overrated junk collector.

"I've been hoping once you had everything working smoothly, you'd join me at church some Sunday." Ms. Ada interrupted her thoughts.

Charlie shifted in her chair. Her grandparents, her parents, had been people of faith. Charlie was not. She saw the world for what it was. "I haven't been to church since Grandma's funeral."

Ms. Ada reached her hand across the table and placed it over Charlie's.

"I know you miss her. She loved you so much. She just wanted you to have some peace in your life, a place that felt like home."

Tears unexpectedly welled up in Charlie's eyes.

"Maybe some people don't ever find a real home."

Ms. Ada squeezed Charlie's hand. "I refuse to believe that. Home is anywhere we make it. Give it time. Holiday Cove has a lot to offer."

"Right now, I wish it would offer us some supper. How long have we been sitting here?"

Ms. Ada looked around the diner. "I think Lila has forgotten about us."

"It's so busy, she's probably got more tables than she can handle," Charlie said.

Ms. Ada smiled. "It just gives us more time to chat."

A few minutes later, Lila returned to the table with a basket of biscuits and two glasses of iced tea.

"I apologize. The kitchen is backed up, and they lost your orders. Everything should be up all nice and hot in a few minutes. And as a thank you for your patience, I added two slices of our homemade apple pie on the house."

"Sweet girl, it's not your fault, and we're enjoying catching up. So don't you worry about a thing," Ms. Ada said.

Charlie looked at Lila. She looked as if she had been running a marathon. Beads of sweat covered her forehead, and she was out of breath. She'd make sure to leave a good tip for the poor girl regardless of the lateness of the food arriving.

As promised, a few minutes later, two piping hot plates of food arrived followed by the best apple pie Charlie had ever tasted. Charlie and Ms. Ada lingered over a cup of coffee while Lila boxed the leftovers. Charlie insisted on paying for the meal and walked Ms. Ada to her car.

"I look forward to seeing you tomorrow." Charlie hugged her friend goodbye.

She was glad she had walked. She needed to work off some of the copious amounts of calories she had just consumed.

Charlie could hear Mr. Bear barking from the yard, and it wasn't his usual friendly bark. She ran up the stairs to find him pacing in his kennel. When he saw her come in the room, he began to whine and paw at the door. Charlie quickly let him out and swooped him up in her arms. He wiggled and licked her face. She put him down and checked his kennel to make sure nothing had climbed in there with him. Holiday Cove had its fair share of critters this time of year. She saw nothing out of the ordinary but decided to change his bedding out anyway.

"You've been such a good boy. Do you want a biscuit?"

He jumped up on his hind legs and did a little hop.

There were several words he recognized, and "biscuit" was one of them. They headed into the kitchen and Charlie pulled a box of dog biscuits from the pantry. He took the treat and pitter-pattered his way out of the kitchen to his bed. Charlie was exhausted from her long day. She was going to take a quick shower and then go straight to bed. She noticed the light on in the guest bedroom that doubled as her home office. She could have sworn she turned the light off before she left for dinner. The hair on the back of her neck tingled as she rushed into the room. Nothing look disturbed, but someone had been here. The lockbox with all her secrets was gone. She searched the room like a mad woman, then went through every room in the house but the box was nowhere to be found. Kevin Wilson hadn't been acting alone. He had a partner, and that meant Charlie's secret wasn't safe.

Eight

Charlie hadn't slept at all. She just kept thinking that someone was out that knew everything about her. The letters had threatened exposure of her past sins; things that people would judge and condemn her for. Charlie wasn't naive. She knew the letters were leading to blackmail. The partner could demand almost anything from her now. That lockbox gave her motive for killing Kevin. As much as she wanted to grab Mr. Bear and leave Holiday Cove in the dust, she was stuck. She couldn't leave as long as Kevin's murder remained unsolved. She dragged herself into the kitchen to look for something to eat and groaned when she remembered her invitation to Ms. Ada. Unless all she wanted to serve for dinner was coffee and pork rinds, she needed to figure something out. She was hoping for a busy

Saturday so she wouldn't have time to shop or cook. She'd call Jill at the Cool Cucumber, a small grocery store with a vegetarian only lunch counter. Saturday's special was Jill's homemade eggplant parmesan. Charlie could leave work on her lunch break and pick it up along with some fresh bread and Tiramisu for dessert. It shouldn't take more than a few minutes.

She completed her morning routines and headed downstairs with Mr. Bear. She knew she wouldn't have time to change clothes before dinner so she found a cream linen Armani suit that would suffice. The wide leg pants covered her sandaled feet, and the matching sleeveless vest would be cool on such a hot day. The silk cami underneath helped deflect the scratchiness of the material. She had left her hair natural this morning, and little curls of fire flowed over her shoulders and down her back. She donned a pair of large gold hoop earrings and then found Mr. Bear a cream bowtie covered with little palm trees.

As Charlie turned the lights on downstairs, she wondered about the gun. Where was it? Had Kevin found it or the police? If Kevin's partner had it, the nails were in her coffin. Someone had all the evidence Lance would need to make Charlie his one and only suspect. She needed to find out more about Kevin Wilson, and that meant she'd need to talk to Brett. Susan seemed to know him pretty well, so she'd pump her for information first.

Charlie finished turning on all the lights and went into the kitchen to put on a pot of coffee for the others when they arrived. A few minutes later, Susan appeared in the kitchen.

"I come bearing gifts!" She placed a dozen of Hal's maple toffee donuts on the table.

"That should put the troops in good spirits." Charlie began pouring some coffee.

"They've worked hard this week," Susan said. "I think you've had a successful grand opening."

Charlie sat down with the mugs and slid Susan's over to her as they devoured the delicious donuts.

"Except for the business with Kevin, you're right. I couldn't have asked for better."

"You're still worried, and you shouldn't be. No one thinks you had anything to do with what happened to him."

"Why wouldn't they?" Charlie asked. "Besides Brett, I'm the only person that seems to have really known him."

"I don't think Brett knows much about him either. He saw someone in need and tried to help."

Charlie noticed the blush in Susan's cheek and the slight smile forming on the corner of her lips.

"How well do you know Brett? " Charlie arched an eyebrow.

Susan's blush deepened. "We go to the same church, the one next door that Betty Ann went to. He's always helped those less fortunate than him. He asked for prayer for Kevin once in Sunday school because he was down on his luck."

"Do you remember when this was?" Charlie inquired.

Susan thought for a minute. "I think around Christmas. Kevin had just come to town and was looking for work. Brett had told him about the project here, but that was still a few weeks away at the time. We took up a collection and paid for him a room at Ms. Lou's until he could start work."

"Do you mean Ms. Lou that has the farm next to Andy's?"

"That's her. After her husband died, she turned the bunkhouse into rooms for rent. Her main renters were the extra help the surrounding farmers hired during the summer and fall. But she took Kevin in as a favor to Brett."

Charlie looked confused. "But I thought Kevin was murdered in the valley, not at Ms. Lou's."

Susan shrugged. "He probably got his own place after he started making money. Ms. Lou is kind of strict."

Charlie stared at her empty coffee cup. She'd make a visit to see Ms. Lou tomorrow.

"I know I've left you in charge of things a lot these past few days, but I have one more errand I need to run today. Ms. Ada is bringing her daughter and granddaughter by this afternoon to see the shop, and they're staying for dinner. I've got to pick up the food at Jill's on my lunch break."

"It's no problem," Susan replied. "We have plenty of help, and I look forward to seeing Ms. Ada."

"If you don't have plans for the evening, I'd love for you to join us for dinner."

"I wish I could, but I'm volunteering at the fireworks tent tonight. Our church does it as our fundraising project every year. This year the proceeds go to the food bank. You should come by after dinner. I'll be there until the tent closes down at midnight."

"When do you rest?" Charlie marveled at her assistant.

Susan laughed. "It's more fun than work, and I won't be there by myself. A few others from my Sunday school class volunteered for this shift as well."

"Like Brett?" Charlie teased.

This time there was no mistaking the look on Susan's face.

"Yes. Like Brett and others." Susan left the kitchen before having to answer any more of Charlie's questions.

Charlie stifled a chuckle. Susan definitely had a crush on Brett. Charlie made her after dinner plans to visit the fireworks tent.

The morning went by quickly, and before Charlie knew it, it was lunchtime. Usually, she'd just walk to Jill's store since it was only a few blocks up Main Street, but she was on a tight schedule today with no room for such pleasantries. Thankfully, there was an empty parking spot right in front of the store.

No one really thought a grocery store carrying only organic foods and meatless alternatives would take off in Holiday Cove, but Jill and Toby Landry had made it a success. Buying all their produce from local farmers had helped build ties with the community. But the old-fashioned lunch counter was what had made the biggest impression. The couple had set up a small bar at the back of the store with enough stools to feed ten guests at a time. And it was always full. Jill was a classically trained chef. She served only vegetarian dishes, that were all homemade and all delicious. Every day she had a different special and every day she'd usually sell out. She also did a good take and bake business. She'd make a few extra servings of whatever the daily special was and sell it in family size pans that could be taken home and cooked.

The little bell over the door chimed as Charlie walked in. The aroma of fresh Italian cooking filled the air. Jill greeted Charlie with a wave and a smile from the lunch counter.

"Hey, Charlie! Give me a couple of minutes, and I'll run get your pan from the back."

"Thanks, Jill. I need to pick up a few more things so I'll meet you at the register when I'm done."

Charlie picked up a big head of Romaine lettuce, some shredded parmesan, and a bottle of Jill's homemade Caesar dressing for a quick salad, a loaf of Italian bread, and a batch of Tiramisu for dessert. By the time she had finished shopping, Jill was waiting for her at the cash register.

"Did you find everything you needed?" Jill asked as she placed the pan of eggplant parmesan with Charlie's other items.

"I did, thank you. It's always hard to stick to my list when I come in here."

Jill laughed. "I take that as a compliment. How are things going with your shop?"

"Better than I could have hoped for. It's been a busy few days, which is why you're the lifesaver for tonight's dinner."

"I understand things can get hectic. I was sorry to hear about that awful business with that boy that harassed you. Then for him to be found murdered. You must be under a great deal of stress."

Charlie gave Jill a tight smile and changed the subject.

"Oh my! I almost forgot the olives."

"I'll get them for you." Jill grabbed a jar and finished ringing up Charlie's order without further conversation.

Charlie thanked her and made her way back to the shop. She knew Jill's comment was meant to be harmless, but it reminded her that now everything she did would have a cloud of suspicion around it. As she put the groceries away in the downstairs kitchen, she promised herself she would not go through that again.

nine

Ms. Ada, her daughter, Elizabeth, and granddaughter, Hannah, showed up promptly at four. Susan ushered them into the downstairs kitchen where Charlie was just putting the eggplant parmesan in the oven.

Charlie rushed to hug Ms. Ada, who looked like she just stepped off the set of an old movie. A red turban covered her white hair and matched the flowing red dress and robe that ended just above her ankles. Shiny gold gladiator sandals adorned her feet. Gold bangles ran up both arms, and a pair of gold chandelier earrings hung from her lobes. Her red lips burst into a proud smile as she introduced Elizabeth and Hannah to Charlie.

Elizabeth was the opposite of her mother. She wore almost no makeup or jewelry. She wore plain white trousers and a peach blouse with a sensible pair of loafers. Her brown hair was cut into a stylish bob. Charlie guessed she was in her early fifties. Hannah, however, seemed to lean towards her grandmother's choice of bright colors in a yellow sundress and rainbow streaks running through her choppy blonde hair. The teenager had finished off her outfit with a pair of multi-colored high tops.

"It's so nice to meet you both. I hope you're hungry. We'll be eating soon." Charlie led them out of the kitchen and into the store. Mr. Bear woke up as they passed by. Hannah squealed in delight when she saw him.

"He's so cute!"

She reached down to pet him, and the dog stood up on his hind legs with his front paws out as if asking to be held. Hannah obliged and cradled him in her arms as they began the tour.

Ms. Ada's eyes twinkled as Charlie escorted them through the big showroom and library, but the hit of the tour was the clothes. Charlie smiled as Hannah tried to shop with one hand because she wouldn't let go of Mr. Bear. Ms. Ada rummaged through the jewelry like a pirate looking for buried treasure. A row of vintage Halston dresses had caught Elizabeth's eye. Charlie let them shop without interruption until Susan came in.

"I've sent the girls home and locked everything up. And I turned the oven off so you won't burn dinner."

Charlie looked down at watch. It was past five. They had been having so much fun, Charlie had lost track of time.

"Susan, you're a lifesaver. I don't know what I'd do without you."

Susan laughed. "Well, today you would have burned down your kitchen. Don't forget to come by the fireworks tent later if you get bored."

"Deal! Now go have some fun. I'll see you later."

Charlie turned back to her guests. They all had several items, and Susan had shut down the registers.

"Charlie, you have such good taste," Ms. Ada beamed. "I could spend an afternoon here."

"Me too!" Hannah agreed. She held a bundle of clothes in one hand and Mr. Bear in the other.

"Where do you find such quality pieces?" Elizabeth asked.

"It's easier now than it used to be. People aren't holding on to things anymore. I get lots of calls about estate sales where heirs are just selling off what is left to them. And I go on several trips a year looking for unique items."

"You have a fascinating job, and you seem to do it well. I'm glad mother had us come by today."

Charlie was pleased with Elizabeth's praise. "Thank you. I'm afraid Susan has already closed the registers, but if y'all are okay with hand printed receipts, I can go ahead and tally everything up for you."

"Charlie, put everything on my bill and I'll write you a check," Ms. Ada said over her protesting daughter.

Charlie did as she was told and handed Ms. Ada the bill. After everything was squared away, the foursome and

Mr. Bear made their way upstairs with the eggplant parmesan for dinner. The meal was perfect, and the conversation was warm and welcoming. Elizabeth, Ms. Ada, and Charlie lingered over coffee and tiramisu while Hannah played with Mr. Bear in the living room.

"Betty Ann would be proud of what you've done with the place." Ms. Ada reached over the table and grasped Charlie's hand. "You were always the bright light in her life. She suffered so much with the loss of your parents and grandfather. But she always smiled when she'd talk about you and your adventures."

Charlie felt a twinge of guilt. She should have visited more. Her grandmother had given her a place to live after her parents' car accident in Germany. She had put aside her own grief to help Charlie deal with hers. Betty Ann had held tightly to her faith while Charlie had lost hers.

"She was better to me than I deserved."

Ms. Ada gripped Charlie's hand. "She held no ill feelings toward you, child. She knew you were doing the best you could out there on your own."

Elizabeth quietly left the room as Ms. Ada, and Charlie continued to talk. The stress of the last few days overwhelmed Charlie, and she became undone at the kind woman's offer of comfort.

"I couldn't get out of here fast enough when I turned eighteen. I didn't listen to her advice or take into consideration she needed me to stay. I was selfish and angry. I didn't want anything to do with her God or with her faith. She would be ashamed if she knew all the mistakes I've made. Ms. Ada, your words are sweet, and I appreciate you saying them. But they're not true. My grandmother would be anything but proud of me."

Tears streamed down Charlie's face, and her body shook with uncontrollable sobs. Ms. Ada rose from her seat and went to Charlie, enveloping her in a hug.

"Sweet, sweet girl. You are just eaten up with guilt, aren't you? Your grandmother's love was fashioned after God's love for us. It wasn't dependent on your actions. She loved you, no matter what. There was nothing you could have done to change the way she felt about you. That's the way God loves us, too, dear. Nothing can separate us from his love."

Charlie hadn't cried this much since Betty Ann's funeral. But she cried herself out now, safe in Ms. Ada's arms. She took a few deep breaths and wiped her tear-stained face with a napkin. She didn't know if she believed what Ms. Ada was saying, but it felt good to release some of the tension she had been feeling. She stood up from her chair and hugged her friend.

"Thank you. I think I needed a good old-fashioned cry."

Ms. Ada smiled. "It does do a world of good from time to time, doesn't it? Now, let's go see how badly my daughter and granddaughter have spoiled Mr. Bear."

The two women walked into the living room to find Hannah snuggled up on the couch, asleep with Mr. Bear in her arms. Elizabeth sat on the other end of the sofa, reading a home decor magazine she had found on the coffee table.

"I don't feel like a very good hostess leaving you two to fend for yourselves while I monopolized your mother's time."

"Don't be silly! This has been a wonderful evening. Although I don't know how you're going to separate these two," she said, pointing to Hannah and Mr. Bear. "They've played themselves out."

The women laughed as Elizabeth woke Hannah. Mr. Bear bounced up and went to grab a toy, ready for another game of keep away. The small group chatted for a few more minutes before saying their goodbyes, then Charlie escorted them downstairs. By the time she cleaned up, it was after eight, and she was physically tired and emotionally drained. She called Susan and told her she wouldn't be making it to the firework stand that night. Instead, she was going to take a nice hot bath and go to bed early.

She sank into the old clawfoot tub, the bubbles and hot water coming to her chin. She picked apart the events of the last couple of days, trying to think who could have killed Kevin. She must have dozed off because the next thing she knew the alarm was going off downstairs. She could hear Mr. Bear frantically barking and running up and down the hall outside her door. She barely dried off before putting on a robe and slippers. She grabbed the ringing phone. The alarm company let her know they were sending the police and to stay where she was, but Charlie was already heading down the stairs. She crept through the kitchen and into the hallway. She noticed her office door open. There was no way she could have left it open because the alarm wouldn't set unless it was closed. She was walking toward the office when the floorboard behind her creaked. She turned around in time to see a glimpse of a masked figure. It was the last thing she saw before everything went black.

Ten

Moll! Moll! Can you hear me? "

Charlie tried to open her eyes. What was Andy doing in her house?

"No! Don't move. Help is coming."

"Andy?"

"Yeah, Hon, it's me. Just be still, okay? I'm going to be right back. I need to find something to stop the bleeding."

Charlie tried to open her eyes again. Her head felt like it was on fire. She reached to rub her temples and felt a sticky substance. Her eyes finally focused, and she looked at her fingers. They were covered with blood. Andy reappeared from the kitchen and sat down on the floor beside her.

"I need you to be real still, Hon. I'm gonna move your head just a little."

She wanted to tell him to cut the southern gentleman routine and quit calling her "Hon," but the words wouldn't come out of her mouth. Andy laid her head gently in his lap. He had taken some dishcloths from the kitchen and wetted them down with warm water. She cried out in pain as Andy pressed the cloth against her head.

"Shhh, I know it hurts, but I've gotta stop the bleeding."

Charlie gritted her teeth and let him tend to her wound.

"Police!" Someone shouted from the front of the house.

"We're in here!" Andy shouted. "Help!"

An officer ran into the hall. He immediately called for an ambulance.

"What happened here?"

"I don't know," Andy answered. "This is my friend's house. I was walking into the Dining Car when I heard the alarm going off. I ran over, and the front door was open. I found her like this. She's been hit in the head with something, and it won't stop bleeding.

"Andy!" Nan rushed into the room, followed by Lance. She knelt down beside Charlie.

"Hey! Looks like Andy's been taking good care of you. You've given us a little excitement this evening, haven't you?"

Charlie grabbed Nan's hand as the paramedics entered.

"Ma'am, we need you to move so we can take a look at her." One of the paramedics helped Nan off the floor.

The other took her place beside Charlie. He asked her some questions and shined a light in her eyes.

"Do you think you can move?" he asked.

"Yes. Help me up, please." Charlie answered.

The first paramedic had returned with a stretcher, but Charlie waved him away.

"I don't need that. Just give me a minute."

"Charlie, let them help you." Andy insisted.

"I'm fine!" Charlie snapped, "Just get me off this floor!"

The paramedic and Andy helped Charlie into the kitchen with Nan and Lance following behind.

Charlie refused to go to the hospital, so the paramedics left after giving her instructions to avoid falling asleep for the next few hours and urging her to visit her doctor first thing Monday morning. Nan was furious that Charlie wouldn't go.

"Charlie Ann Flynn! You're being stubborn! You could have a concussion, for goodness sakes!"

"I don't have a concussion. I have a headache, and you yelling at me is not helping it."

Nan's heels made a staccato sound on the tile as she marched to the freezer to get Charlie more ice for her head.

"At least Andy was here. You could have been murdered if he hadn't shown up."

Charlie smiled at Andy. "She's right about that. I'm glad you were close by."

Lance interjected. "Yeah, Officer Lewis said you heard the alarm from the Dining Car. Nan and I were inside, and we didn't hear anything. We wouldn't have known anything was going on if I hadn't gotten called by one of the officers on scene."

The Dining Car was Holiday Cove's fanciest restaurant. Years ago, a semi-retired French chef Henry Granger, bought the old abandoned train depot in the center of town. He renovated the depot and turned it into a train museum, then brought in a refurbished rail car that he turned into an upscale French restaurant. It was ridiculously expensive and only open for dinner. The Dining Car was a favorite place for couples and special occasions, so it was an odd place for a bachelor like Andy to have dinner on a Saturday night.

"I was getting out of my car when I heard the alarm, so I just got back in and rushed over here."

"I hope your date didn't get mad," Lance said.

Andy averted Charlie's gaze. "I texted her to explain. No big deal."

"Did you see anything or anyone when you got here?" Lance asked.

Andy shook his head. "Just the open door and the mess in the office."

"What mess in the office?" Charlie demanded.

The others hesitated in answering. Charlie got up from her chair and walked toward the office. She ignored the officers collecting fingerprints and taking pictures. She held back tears as she surveyed the destruction. Paperwork and files covered the floor, shelves were knocked over, and broken glass, books, and boxes of merchandise were strewn around the room. Her office chair was broken, and two leather club chairs had been gutted, their stuffing bursting through the seams. Red spray paint splattered the walls with the words MURDERER over and over. Charlie's lips quivered, and she clenched her fist as rage filled her mind and body. Nan put her arms around her shoulder.

"Why don't you get Mr. Bear and come stay with us tonight?"

Charlie took a deep breath. "I won't be run out of my own home. How much longer is this going to take? I want to start cleaning up."

"We're almost done," one of the techs answered.

Charlie didn't say anything as she walked back into the kitchen. She put on a pot of coffee, trying to keep herself busy.

As the others sat back down, Lance cleared his throat.

"Charlie, besides Kevin Wilson, do you know of anyone who might think of you as an enemy?"

Only one. And he was nowhere near Holiday Cove. But someone knew about him, knew about her, and what she'd done. Kevin had known. She just had to figure out who his partner was. That was her enemy. She put a cup of coffee down in front of Lance.

"Almost all the people I know in this town are right here in this room. And to my knowledge, none of you think of me as an enemy."

"What about anyone outside of Holiday Cove? You were away from here for a lot of years." Lance persisted.

"If I wasn't here, I was on the road," Charlie said. "It was a solitary life, not a lot of chances to make friends. Or enemies."

"No relationships in twenty years?" Lance asked. "I hate to dig into your personal life, I really do. But I got an unsolved murder here, and everything points to you knowin' something about it, so I need you to be honest with me."

Andy placed his hand on Charlie's. "I think that's enough for now. She's not in the best condition to be answering questions."

Lance stared at Andy. "Are you speakin' as her attorney or her friend?"

"Both. If you want to be here as a friend and talk to her about what happened tonight, then that's one thing. But interrogating her to find out more information on a murder investigation is another. You need to do that in an official capacity, not here at her dining room table."

Lance stood up, his face turning scarlet. "Listen up, Counselor. I've been lenient out of respect to Nan and Charlie's friendship. But the truth is, I think she's holdin' out on me. Nobody has any idea what she's been up to for the last decade. And if you push me or question my motives again, I will haul your client in for questioning right now. Do I make myself clear?"

Nan gasped. "Lance! We know Charlie. Quit treating her like a criminal and apologize!"

Before Lance could respond, Charlie held up her hand. "It's okay. It's been a crazy few days, and he's just doing his job. But I think it's best you both leave. If you have further questions for me, then contact Andy for a formal request. I'm done talking."

"It goes without saying, but don't leave town. You'll be hearing from me soon." Lance stomped from the room. They could hear him barking orders to the techs to finish up.

Nan hugged Charlie. "I'm so sorry, sweetie. You know I'm here for you. If you need anything, please call me, okay?"

Charlie nodded. Nan turned to Andy. "You take care of our girl. If anything happens to her, you'll have me to answer to."

"I'll take care of her. I promise," Andy said.

One of the techs came into the kitchen. "We're done, Ms. Flynn."

Charlie offered a weak smile. "Thank you."

She followed the tech out of the kitchen to take another look at the office. Along with the mess, fingerprint dust now covered most of the surfaces in the once immaculate office. She came back to the kitchen to find Andy rifling through the kitchen cabinets.

"What are you doing?" She asked.

Andy turned around. "Trying to find some cleaning supplies. I figured I'd try to tidy up the office as best as I could, but you're probably going to need someone to paint it."

Charlie shook her head. "You're not cleaning my office at ten-thirty at night in those clothes."

"What's wrong with my clothes?" He asked as he straightened his tie and suit jacket.

"You're dressed for a date, not house cleaning. Go home. I'm going to get some sleep. I'll tackle this fiasco in the morning."

Andy ignored the jab about the date. "The paramedic said you needed to stay awake a couple of hours."

"I will," Charlie said. "But, for now, I'm going upstairs, changing into my pj's, and checking on Mr. Bear. I will call you if I need anything."

Andy knew the look. There was no use arguing. "Call me first thing when you wake up. No excuses."

Charlie nodded. "I promise."

She walked him to the door, locked it, and turned on the alarm before going back upstairs. She watched Andy get into his truck and wondered for the umpteenth time who his date was and why it bothered her that he had one. Just another thought she needed to push to the back of her mind. Tomorrow was a big day. She was going to find out more about Kevin Wilson and why someone was convinced she'd murdered him.

Eleven

The morning sun flooded the living room with light. Charlie groaned in discomfort as she tried to move. She had stayed awake until after two in the morning and had fallen asleep on the couch. Her head ached, and her muscles were sore. She wanted nothing more than to close the curtains, get in her comfy bed, and sleep the day away, but she had to find out more about Kevin. Ms. Lou's farm was at least a thirty-minute drive out of town. She decided to take the old yellow VW bug still sitting in the garage. She had only driven it a few times since her grandmother's death because she preferred the conveniences of her truck. But today would be a perfect day for a drive in the country with the top down. She needed some fresh air to clear the cobwebs from her brain. She'd even take Mr. Bear with her. He'd love a Sunday morning drive. Her head was still tender, so she grabbed a scarf and placed it gently over her curls. Maybe that would be enough to keep the wind from making a rat's nest of her hair. She didn't bother with make-up, but she did smack on a little nude lip gloss so her grandmother wouldn't roll over in her grave. She found the perfect sky-blue gingham romper and white espadrilles to complete the sunny day vibe she was going for.

She poured herself a large coffee, found her keys and a pair of black over-sized sunglasses, and made her way to the garage. She was thankful she had kept the little seventies VW in good repair. Mr. Bear wiggled impatiently as she buckled him in. He loved rides. She put the top down and turned on the radio to a golden oldies station. She could almost feel her grandmother's presence. Betty Ann loved nothing more than a Sunday outing after church. Charlie stopped at a drive through and got a biscuit to quiet her rumbling stomach. Mr. Bear barked at the girl at the window until she gave him a treat, then they were on the road. Charlie sang along to the radio with Mr. Bear joining in with a bark from time to time. Soon she was at Ms. Lou's farm.

Long rows of corn grew on either side of the gravel drive. Closer to the old rambling farmhouse was a grand garden full of green beans, lettuce, carrots, peppers, and a multitude of other vegetables. Ms. Lou was at one of the outer rows chucking green beans into a basket. Charlie guessed the dainty gardener was in her late seventies. Baggy overalls enveloped her small frame, and a large straw hat hid almost all of her delicate features and curly white hair. She stood up and removed her gloves when she saw Charlie and Mr. Bear approaching.

"Well, what do we have here?" She smiled as Mr. Bear pranced around on his leash.

"Good morning, my name is Charlie Flynn, and this shy little fella is Mr. Bear."

"Flynn, you say? I knew a Betty Ann Flynn."

Charlie smiled. "That was my grandmother."

"Sad to hear of her passin'. Seems I do remember somethin' about a granddaughter. Well, don't just stand there. They'd take away my old southern lady card if I didn't offer you some lemonade and sugar cookies. I might even be able to track down somethin' for your furry friend there."

"Oh, I don't want to impose," Charlie said. "I just had a few questions about an old resident of yours: Kevin Wilson."

The smile on Ms. Lou's face dropped for the tiniest of moments, but she regained it quickly. "Nonsense. We'll eat and talk at the same time. Go sit at that old picnic table, and I'll be right back. If the dog will behave and stay out of my garden, you're welcome to let him run."

Charlie looked down at Mr. Bear. "I'm trusting you to be good. Stay away from the garden, and I'll let you loose."

He barked his consent and Charlie let him off his leash. He ran ahead, sniffing the ground in excitement. Charlie sat at the little picnic table shaded by a giant oak tree as she watched Mr. Bear chase a butterfly. Soon, Ms. Lou emerged from the house with a tray of the promised beverage and cookies. Charlie took a sip of the lemonade as Ms. Lou gave Mr. Bear a pig ear to chew on. He took his treat to the far end of the table and began to gnaw on it.

"Now, what do you want to know about Kevin?" Ms. Lou munched on a cookie as Charlie took another sip of refreshing lemonade.

"Nobody seems to know much about him, so when I found out he used to live here, I thought I'd see if you could remember anything."

"Just because I live out here in the country don't mean I don't hear things," Ms. Lou said. "Seems you and he had a bit of a row before he passed. That got anything to do with your interest in him?"

Charlie wasn't going to lie. "Yes, ma'am, it does. Because of that disagreement, I feel like there are people that have questions about my involvement in his murder. Last night, someone broke into my home, attacked me, and trashed my office. I plan to find out everything I can about this man so I can clear my name."

Ms. Lou grinned. "How many times people tell you that you're the spittin' image of your mamma?"

Charlie was shaken by the sudden change of subject and the mention of her mother.

"To be honest, most people don't talk to me about her. They talk more about my grandmother."

"Oh, I see some Betty Ann in ya too, but that spark fire you got goin' on. That's all your mamma. She'd set her jaw just like you did right there and fire would fly from her

eyes when she got all riled and righteous. Taught her Sunday
school class for years. I've seen that look more than my fair
share. She had a strong head for what was wrong and what
was right. And there wasn't no changing her mind, that's for
sure."

Charlie felt comforted by Ms. Lou's recollection of her
mother. "The world was black and white for her. And
you're right, she didn't back down from anyone or
anything."

Ms. Lou took another bite of cookie before she spoke
again. "I always liked your mamma. So, I'll tell ya what you
want to know, but I don't think it's gonna help ya none."

"Thank you," Charlie said. "Anything you tell me is
more than I know now."

"That Kevin was a nasty fella," Ms. Lou made a face.
"But I don't think Brett knew that when he sent him to me.
He was just tryin' to be charitable. But from the first minute
that boy got here, he was trouble. I have strict rules for
these young men, and they follow 'em, or they get gone. It's
that simple. Since I don't get to go to church no more, we
read the Bible and pray every Sunday morning, and I fix a
big breakfast. Then, they have the rest of the day to
themselves. It never failed, Kevin would always have an
excuse not to show up for Bible time, but when it came to
free time, he was always ready. I don't allow no drinkin',
smokin', or girls 'round here. More than once, I think he
snuck in all three. I hate to admit it, but he was just too
tricky for me to catch. Then things started goin' missin', and

there was a big fight between him and another one of my boys. That boy gave Kevin a mighty beatin'. Wasn't long after that, Kevin left."

"The boy that beat Kevin is he still here?" Charlie asked.

Ms. Lou shook her head. "Sorry, Vincent is one of my success stories. I gave him one more chance after the fight with Kevin. He straightened up real good. Got him a construction job over in Knoxville. He's stayin' outta trouble, going to church, and even got himself a girlfriend."

Charlie was disappointed but smiled at Ms. Lou anyway. "You've been very helpful. And that lemonade was the best I've ever had."

Ms. Lou beamed. "Oh, you know who you might want to talk to is Andy Brock. Kevin helped him out a few times. Last time he was over there, he came back with a black eye."

Charlie wondered why Andy had never mentioned this to her. She passed the road to his farm on the way in. She'd stop by on her way out. After wrangling Mr. Bear away from his pig ear and into the car, she promised Ms. Lou another visit.

Charlie drove down the long dirt road that led to Andy's farm. She was playing with the radio and almost hit another car barreling down the narrow road. She saw it in time to swerve back on her side. The other driver didn't even slow down. She tried to catch a glimpse of the car to see if she recognized it, but all she saw was a cloud of dust. She wondered who else was visiting Andy this morning.

Could it have been his mysterious date from last night? Charlie felt an unbidden pang of jealousy and scolded herself mentally. The last thing she need was a romantic entanglement, especially with the likes of Andy.

The Brock farm could have been a painting. A big red barn loomed on the horizon, and in front of it stood a pristine, two-story farmhouse with black shutters and a wraparound porch. A large herd of cattle grazed on green fields of grass dotted with yellow dandelions. In the other field, spotted ponies ran and played in the warming afternoon sun. Andy's blue truck was parked in front of the barn. Gus ran from his napping place as soon as he heard Charlie's VW coming up the drive. Mr. Bear popped up from his seat and greeted his friend with a hearty bark. Gus wagged his tail and barked in excitement as Charlie and Mr. Bear got out of the car. Andy stepped out of the barn but lacked Gus's enthusiasm at the sight of his visitors. His silver hair and the front of his t-shirt were wet with perspiration. His jeans were covered with dirt and oil. An old tractor sat in the barn, its hood up, various tools littering the ground.

"Shouldn't you be home resting?" Andy asked.

"Hello to you, too," Charlie shot back.

Andy took a rag from his back pocket and wiped his face.

"Sorry, I've got a lot to do today, and my trusty old tractor isn't being so trusty."

"I about had a head-on collision with your other visitor on the way up here. If it was your date from last night, I hope you got things ironed out."

Andy leaned against the truck and squinted at Charlie.

"What's the sudden interest in my love life? You've never cared before."

Charlie shrugged. "Maybe because you've never been so secretive about it before. And speaking of secrets, why didn't you tell me that you knew Kevin and that he worked for you on the farm? Or why didn't you mention the black eye he left here with?"

Andy raised his chin. "I hear an accusation somewhere in there, Moll. What kind of lawyer do you think I am?"

Charlie got defensive. "I'm not worried about what kind of lawyer you are as much as I'm concerned about what kind of friend you are. You could have told me you knew him. And stop calling me Moll! I'm not a gangster!"

"As you wish, Ms. Flynn, and for the record, I didn't know Kevin!" Andy threw the rag to the ground. "He was one of four or five guys that helped around last year with some remodeling I was doing on the house."

"Ms. Lou said he was trouble," Charlie said. "Are you telling me nothing happened here?"

Andy stared at Charlie for a minute and walked back into the barn.

"Believe me or don't. I have work to do." Andy turned his back and started working on the tractor, leaving Charlie standing speechless. She regained her composure, picked up Mr. Bear, and marched to the car.

"Thanks for nothing!" She yelled as she slammed the car door and peeled out of the driveway. It looked like she was going to need a new lawyer.

Twelve

harlie gripped the steering so hard her knuckles were white. Her Ray-Bans hid a death scowl, and a ball of rage settled into the pit of her stomach. Andy was hiding something from her, and she was hurt and angry. He was supposed to be her friend. She could count on one hand the people she trusted, so losing one was devastating. And to be dismissed like that was not like Andy. As she was coming back up the highway into town, she saw the big fireworks tent in front of the superstore. She wondered if Susan and Brett were there. She pulled into the parking lot. Luckily, it wasn't too crowded. She and Mr. Bear entered the tent. It was filled with every firework imaginable. Red, white, and blue bunting around the tables gave the tent a festive look. A massive table in the center highlighted the biggest box of fireworks she had ever seen. Anyone who bought that was going to put on one heck of a show. The checkout area was to her right. A small group of people in matching red shirts sat in a semi-circle behind the cash register. Susan saw her approaching and gave her a wave.

"Charlie! Mr. Bear! This is a pleasant surprise!"

Mr. Bear began wagging his tail and jumping up and down on his front paws as soon as he heard Susan's voice.

"Charlie! What is that big bump on your head?" Susan asked.

Charlie told her about the break-in and the assault.

"You should have called me, but I'm just glad you're okay."

"Me too. Are you and Brett getting a break anytime soon? I'd like to take you to lunch."

"Our shift was over an hour ago. We've just been sitting here talking. Where would you like to go?"

"If you're done, why don't y'all just come to the house? I've got some leftover eggplant parmesan. I'll whip up a fresh salad and some garlic bread. There's even half a pan of tiramisu left for dessert. I'd like to talk to Brett about Kevin. I'll catch you up on everything when you get to the house."

Susan looked worried. "Sure. We'll get our things and head on over. See you in about thirty minutes."

The two girls hugged goodbye and Charlie was on her way. She had a few minutes to tidy up and get the food heated before her guests arrived. By the time Charlie heard them coming up the steps, she had everything on the table. She hadn't spoken to Brett since he had finished the job on the Victorian.

"Brett, I know I've said it before, but I couldn't be more pleased with how everything turned out with the house."

The big guy blushed. "Well, I was worried. You and I didn't get off on the best of terms."

Charlie took a good look at him and Susan as they sat across the table. They surely were an odd-looking pair. Brett was a beefy guy with a permanent tan from working outside all the time. This was the first time she'd seen him without a hat, so she had never noticed the white blonde hair that hid beneath it. Susan was dwarfed beside him, and her goth look was in stark contrast to his boy-next-door charm.

"I guess we didn't," Charlie said. "But you had no idea what Kevin was up to."

Brett still seemed bothered by the situation. "No, and if I had known, he sure wouldn't have been on my crew."

"Susan tells me he came to you looking for a job around Christmas. Had you ever seen him around before then?"

Brett thought about it for a minute. "No, I was having breakfast one day at the Chick-n-Hen. He came in looking kind of rough. He picked up a menu there by the cash register then started digging in his pocket. He counted what little money he had and started to walk out the door. I figured he didn't have enough to buy anything to eat. I got his attention before he left and had him come sit with me. We talked, and he asked if I knew of any place he might be able to get a job. I had just signed the contract with you the day before to start work after the holidays. He said he had some experience in construction. I told him it would be a few weeks before I could help him. Then he started telling me this hard luck story. That's why I helped him in the first place."

"Do you remember what his story was?" Charlie asked.

Brett nodded. "He said he'd been traveling with his girlfriend. They stayed a couple of nights at that motor lodge down by the interstate. One night, they were drinking and partying, then got into a big fight. He woke up the next morning, and she was gone. Took the car, all the money, and most of his things. The guy at the lodge kicked him out, so he walked into town. He'd been staying at the Mission. After we talked a little more, I bought his meal and made a call to Ms. Lou. She said she had some work that could tide him over until we started at your house. I sent him to stay there until he could get on his feet."

"Did he ever mention working for Andy?"

"One of the other guys on my crew did. He was staying at Ms. Lou's too. Said he came back from Andy's farm one day with a black eye. Never said what it was for, but the guy thought it was over a girl."

Charlie was surprised. "A girl? I can't believe Andy would hit someone over a girl. Does the man who told you about this still work for you?"

"Yeah, James Robbins. And he's still at Ms. Lou's as far as I know."

"Looks like I'll be making another trip to Ms. Lou's this week," Charlie said. "Thanks for the information. Now, who's up for some Tiramisu?"

"You don't have to ask me twice!" Brett smiled as he held up his empty plate. Charlie gave him an extra helping and poured some more coffee.

"Are you going to talk to Andy about Kevin?" Susan asked.

"I already did," Charlie told Susan about the morning's conversation with him. "I've never known of him to act like that. Maybe there is a girl involved. He didn't want to talk about his date last night either."

"Speaking of last night, what are you going to do about the office?" Susan asked.

Charlie threw her hands up in disgust. "I don't even want to think about! I'll clean it up later and then call someone tomorrow to come and repaint it."

Brett spoke up. "There's no need for that. We can help you this afternoon. I'll call a couple of my guys, and we could have it done for you today. I'll even see if I can reach James. That'll give you a chance to ask him about Kevin and Andy."

"I really couldn't ask y'all to do that," Charlie said. "You worked at the fireworks tent last night and this morning. You both have to be exhausted."

"I think Brett has a great idea," Susan said. "If we work together, we'll have it done in no time."

Charlie relented. "Only if you let me pay them an overtime wage and throw in a free supper."

"I'll take care of the wages, but supper sounds good," Brett agreed.

Charlie laughed. "You're a tough negotiator. Let me clean up here and then we'll tackle the office."

Brett stood up from the table. "I need to go to my house and get my work truck; it's got all my tools in it. I'll get in touch with the guys. We should be back and ready to work in a couple of hours."

Susan walked to the door with Brett. "I'm going to help Charlie with the dishes. I'll see you when you get back."

After tidying up the kitchen, Charlie put Mr. Bear in his kennel with a toy and a treat. Then she and Susan went downstairs to survey the damage to the office in the light of day.

"Oh my gosh!" Susan stood in shock as she looked at the mess. The blood-red paint on the walls gave her chills. "Why would someone do this to you?"

Charlie shook her head. "Someone thinks I killed him and it looks like they want some payback. I just can't figure out who it could be."

"What about the girlfriend?" Susan asked. "She comes back to make up, finds out he's dead, and talk of the town has a finger pointing at you."

"Susan, you're a genius!" Charlie nearly shouted. "I hadn't thought of that. I need to get out to that motel and see if the girlfriend ever came back looking for Kevin."

"Not you!" Susan put her hands on her hips. "You need to talk to Lance and send him. If she happens to be there, the last thing you need is a run in with a girlfriend with a grudge."

Charlie agreed. "You're right. I'll call Lance now and see if he can find out anything. In the meantime, I've got plenty to keep me busy."

Charlie called Lance, and he promised to go out to the motor lodge to check things out. Then Susan and Charlie started clearing the debris from the office. They were almost done when Brett showed up with James and another worker from his crew. They helped move all the furniture and shelving out of the office.

Once that was done, Susan and Charlie drove to the market to get something to feed everyone. By the time the guys were done with the office, they'd be ready for supper. When they got back to the house, Lance's patrol car was sitting in the driveway. He and Brett were in the downstairs kitchen, drinking some iced tea.

"The guys are almost done with the first coat." Brett grabbed a bag of groceries from Susan's arm. "We shouldn't be much longer."

"Thank you, Brett," Charlie said. "Once I get done talking to Lance, I'll start up the grill." Susan started putting groceries away while Charlie sat down at the table.

"Did you get a chance to talk to anyone at the motel?" Charlie asked.

Lance nodded. "Guy by the name of Jonas Wells. He owns the place, lives in a room off the back of the lobby. Says he knows all the comings and goings of the guests. He remembers Kevin and his girlfriend. He hasn't seen either of them since she left him high and dry. I got a description in case she comes back, and Mr. Wells is gonna come down to the station tomorrow and give it to the sketch artist just to make sure she hasn't been lurking around unnoticed. You really think this girlfriend's responsible for this mess here?"

"You saw the office," Charlie said. "That was personal. Who else would care that Kevin was killed or want to make sure your number one suspect didn't get away with it?"

Lance responded to her insinuation. "I'm just doing my job, Charlie. You're the only other person besides Brett that had any motive."

Charlie wanted to say something about Andy and Kevin but wanted to make sure she had all the facts first.

"I know you don't believe me. But I had nothing to do with Kevin's murder."

"I didn't say I didn't believe you," Lance argued. "I said you were holdin' something back. You still are. Trust me; I want you to be innocent. It sure would get me out of the dog house."

Charlie smiled at the thought of little Nan going head to head with big Lance over Charlie. She was a true friend. She may have lost Andy, but she would always have Nan

Holiday. She was a bulldog and wouldn't stop until Charlie's name was restored.

"Then hopefully we'll find out who really killed him before you wind up in divorce court," Charlie teased.

"Not funny," Lance grumbled. "I'll let you know if anything turns up. Try and stay out of trouble in the meantime."

Charlie walked him to his car and then helped Susan with the rest of the dinner preparations. Susan brought out a folding table and chairs from the garage while Charlie started the grill. The guys finished up just as all the burgers were ready. Everyone sat down to eat and talked casually as the sun began to set. Charlie lit a couple of citronella torches to keep the bugs at bay while they finished their meal.

"James, Brett tells me you knew Kevin Wilson," Charlie said. "What did you think of him?"

Charlie could tell the young man had not had an easy life. He looked a good ten years older than the twenty-two years Brett said he was. His nose had been broken at least once, and a scar ran down the right side of his face from the corner of his eye to the top of his lip. He was underweight for his tall frame, and his teeth needed major dental work. But he had a quiet strength about him. Charlie could see why Ms. Lou and Brett trusted him.

The young man put his burger back down on the plate and looked Charlie directly in the eye.

"Ms. Flynn, have you ever lost your way? I mean really lost yourself. One bad choice after another and you're somewhere you never thought you'd be, doing things you never thought you'd do?"

"Like recognizes like," her grandmother had always said. Did this boy recognize that part of her? She didn't answer the question but motioned for him to continue.

"That's how most of us end up at Ms. Lou's. And for us, she's the last stop before we get so lost, we can't find our way back. Kevin was lost like that, but he didn't want to admit it, didn't want to lump himself in with the rest of us. Ms. Lou and Brett here, they offer guys like me a chance at finding themselves again. They give us work, a sense of responsibility. There's a reward in a hard day's work I never understood before. But Kevin, he only wanted to work the system, take the easy way out. Kept bragging about how he was gonna be rich real soon."

"Did he ever mention how he was going to come into all this money?" Charlie asked.

James shook his head. "Nah, just said his old lady had something lined up."

"That's strange," Charlie said. "We were under the impression the girlfriend had left him here."

"Could be it was a different girl," James said. "He fancied himself a lady's man. That's what the fight between him and Mr. Brock was about."

Charlie pressed him. "You're sure it was over a girl?"

"Yes, ma'am!" James said. "A few of us from Ms. Lou's were helping Mr. Brock do some remodeling on that big, old farmhouse. We were taking a break in the kitchen when he walked through with this girl. Kevin's eyes about popped out of his head. He followed them out to the driveway. I heard the girl's car drive away, then Mr. Brock and Kevin start talkin' real loud. I couldn't hear what they were saying exactly. But I figured they were talking about the girl because Mr. Brock warned Kevin to stay away from her. Then they got even louder, yellin' at each other. Me and the other boys peeked outside to see what was happenin'. Kevin said somethin' real nasty I won't repeat. Mr. Brock tried to push by him, but Kevin was mad and took a swing at him. That's when Mr. Brock punched him. Twice. Once on the nose and once to the eye. Told Kevin to get his things and not come back. Wasn't too long after that he left Ms. Lou's."

Charlie had never known Andy to lose his temper like that. "Did you notice anything suspicious about him when he started working at my house?"

James blushed. "I really can't say."

"James, it's okay. You can tell Ms. Flynn." Brett encouraged him.

"Well, I'd catch him staring at you from time to time, but I didn't think much about it," James blushed. "A lot of the guys stared at you. You're awfully pretty. I'm sorry, Ms. Flynn, I'm not trying to be impolite, just trying to tell the truth."

Charlie smiled. "I'm not angry with you, James. I appreciate your honesty. Ms. Lou and Brett are lucky to have you around."

"Oh, no ma'am. Luck doesn't have anything to do with it. That was God giving this ole boy one last chance."

Charlie wasn't so sure God was in the "last chance" business." Thanks again, James. Now, who has room for more dessert?"

By the end of the evening, Charlie was exhausted. Everyone had gone home, and she and Mr. Bear were taking a quick walk around the yard before bedtime. It has been an eventful day. Tomorrow she would begin the search for Kevin's girlfriend. She could hold the key to proving Charlie's innocence.

Thirteen

ll of Holiday Cove was gearing up for the Fourth. Main Street was covered in a sea of red, white, and blue. Charlie and Susan were busy decorating the pink mansion. Red, white, and blue bunting surrounded the wraparound porch. An American flag hung from a pole over the eaves, and patriotic pinwheels lined the sidewalk leading to the Vintage Gypsy. Now Charlie and Susan were busy tying ribbons decorated with stars and stripes on the shrubs and smaller trees around the yard.

Charlie looked at their handiwork once they were finished. "It clashes with the pink, but I think we still may be in the running for the best-decorated store."

"We have until Friday for judging. So we can make changes if we need to," Susan said.

Charlie boxed up the leftover decorations. "We'll stake out the competition later, for now, we better get back in and give the kiddos a hand. It's not even lunchtime, and we're busier than I thought we'd be."

"Hey, Charlie," Lance said as he walked up the sidewalk. "Susan and the others are going to have to manage without for a while. I need you to come to the station with me."

Charlie laughed. "Lance, leave the jokes for the comedians. We've got a ton of work to do today."

Lance shook his head and looked Charlie in the eye. "It's no joke. I need you to come to the station. You're not under arrest, but it is an official questioning, s you're going to want to call Andy."

"I don't need Andy. Let's get this over with," she said. "Susan, please keep an eye out on the store and make sure Mr. Bear behaves. I'll straighten out whatever this is out and be back as soon as I can."

"Don't worry. I'll take care of everything. Are you sure you don't want me to call Andy for you? "

"No. I can handle this myself. Be back soon." Charlie turned her attention back to Lance. "Well, Officer. Are you escorting me, or am I free to find my own way?"

Lance adjusted his Stetson and sighed. "Don't make this more difficult than it already is. Just be there in fifteen minutes."

Charlie did a mock salute. "Yes, sir!"

Lance ignored her as he walked to his car. Charlie waited for him to leave before she ran up the stairs of the back entrance to her apartment. She didn't want to take the chance of running into anyone. She grabbed her purse and keys, but as she headed to the garage, she changed her mind and decided to walk. At this time of day, it would be almost impossible to get a parking spot at the courthouse. It was only a few blocks, and the walk would give her a chance to blow off some steam. She was dressed comfortably enough in an old pair of Converse and denim overalls. She pulled a rubber band out of her pocket and made a messy ponytail on top of her head. She waved at her neighbors and greeted strangers as she made her way to the police station. It occupied the bottom level of the majestic, white courthouse on the square. As a child, Charlie thought it was the White House and would try to get a glimpse of the President when she walked by with her grandmother. Sometimes they would get a sandwich or hotdog from the street vendor on the corner. Then they'd go sit in the old gazebo under the shade trees, and Charlie would wait expectantly for the President to appear. She was a little disappointed when she got older and realized she and her grandmother had not been eating hot dogs on the White House lawn. Today, she walked by the gazebo and gave it a sad smile. Intuition told her that everything she had tried to keep hidden from Betty Ann was about to blow up in her face. She walked down the sidewalk through the basement entrance into the police station. With a population of around ten thousand people and a low crime rate, the Holiday Cove Police Department wasn't very large. She walked to the desk and asked to speak to Lance. A few minutes later, he appeared and escorted her through a large oak double door. They passed a few desks and a couple of offices until they reached a room at the end of the hall. Charlie froze at the door. She closed her eyes as Lance opened the door and waited for her to enter. She took a deep breath and tried to clear her mind, to concentrate on the present.

"After you," Lance let her step into the room first.

She narrowed her eyes at him as she walked to the table. She took the chair facing the two-way mirror. Lance sat down across from her and placed a folder on the table.

He perused the folder silently and then closed it before sliding it over to Charlie. "I'm not here to make you the bad guy, but the evidence keeps piling up against you, and I've been doing this job long enough to know when someone's keepin' something from me."

Charlie didn't open the folder, just sat there with her hands clasped in her lap. "You said you had questions?"

"Tell me about your time in California."

"No."

Lance raised his eyebrow. "It could help get some of my ducks in a row."

"Your ducks aren't my responsibility. I said no." Fire flashed from her eyes.

Lance opened the folder and took out an old newspaper clipping. Charlie dug her fingernails into her palms. Now she knew where the blackmail evidence had ended up.

"Is that you?" He pointed to a grainy photo on the clipping.

"I don't have to answer that."

"You're right, you don't. But to me, that sure does look a lot like you. And you're sitting pretty as can be behind that defendant's table."

Charlie stared blankly at Lance, refusing to look at the photo.

"Do you know a man by the name of Jack Marsden?"

Charlie's face was stone. "Do you have any questions relevant to what's happening in Holiday Cove now?"

Lance slammed the folder down. "Yeah! I have a big question, Charlie. Why didn't you tell me you'd been on trial for murder before?"

"Don't answer that!" Andy walked in. "Lance, you know better than to question her without me here."

Lance shrugged. "Her exact words were that she didn't need you."

Andy stood firm. "Regardless of what she does or doesn't need, you're done questioning her."

Lance shrugged. "Well, Andy, I think that's up to Ms. Flynn."

"Are you charging me with anything?" Charlie asked.

"Not yet. But when we find the gun used to shoot Kevin, I can't say I won't." He opened the folder again. "On an anonymous tip, we searched his place again. That's where we found this clipping and other evidence that Kevin was blackmailing you. That's a motive. You leave now, you look guilty."

Charlie stood up. "I'm not guilty of anything but thinking I could make a life in this backwater town and that anybody here was capable of loyalty. I'm done. Come with the cuffs next time. It's the only way I'll ever speak to you again." Then she turned to Andy. "And you, you're fired! At best, you're a liar, and at worst you belong in that hot seat." She pointed to the chair she just vacated. "Whatever game you're playing at, you just lost!" She stormed out of the room and down the hall.

Andy followed her out to the parking lot.

"Just what was that supposed to mean? You think I'm a liar? A murderer? You think just because I chose to date someone that wasn't you, I'm a bad guy?"

Charlie wheeled around. Their argument was drawing attention, but she didn't care. "You think this is about who you're dating? Could you be anymore egotistical? This is about you lying to me about Kevin. This is about you having a motive to kill him and still representing me without telling me anything about it. You accuse me of keeping secrets? You can add hypocrite to your list of failings, Mr. Brock, and that's just one more reason that I never want to see you again!"

Andy threw his hands in the air. "I'm not going over this again. I was defending myself, and I know your secret! I've known it for years, and so did your grandmother, she wasn't stupid. I've been protecting you! You just don't have enough sense to tell a friend from an enemy!"

The fact that her grandmother knew the most horrific part of her past broke Charlie. She looked at Andy as if she could squash him like a bug, right there on Main Street. "Don't ever come near me again, Andy Brock. You're dead to me!" She walked away and didn't look back.

Fourteen

nan knocked on the door to Charlie's apartment. Charlie yelled from the other side of the door.

"Go away, Nan! I don't want to see you!"

"Charlie Ann Flynn, I am not going anywhere," Nan protested. "You come open this door right now! I will camp outside this apartment till hell freezes over if I have to."

There was no fighting Nan. Better to just let her say her peace and leave. Charlie opened the door and walked back into the living room.

"Does your husband know you're visiting with the enemy, or did he send you over here to sweet talk information out of me?"

"I'm going to pretend I didn't hear that so we can talk like civilized human beings." Nan sat on the couch across from Charlie.

As usual, she was perfect, not a blonde hair out place or spot on her outrageously expensive white Armani sheath. After marrying Lance, Nan had become one of Holiday Cove's wealthiest citizens. But the money hadn't changed anything but the cost of her wardrobe. Nan always had style. She could make a thrift store outfit look like a million dollars. It made sense when Nan opened her own high-end fashion boutique, Couture Closet. Her stubbornness and street smarts made her an astute businesswoman, and the store was a roaring success.

Charlie, on the other hand, was far from perfect. She had done nothing but angry cry since she got back from the police station an hour ago, and what was left of her make-up was a mascara-smeared mess. She had changed into an old oversized t-shirt and yoga pants that were almost threadbare. She curled up in a chair with Mr. Bear and waited for Nan to speak.

"I don't want to talk about Lance or the case," Nan said. "I just want to make sure you're okay. I heard you and Andy had a shouting match in the middle of the street. Really? That doesn't sound like you."

"Have you ever thought that maybe you don't really know me?" Charlie demanded. "I mean we were friends as kids and teenagers, but now we're grown-ups. We've been apart for years. Do you really call that a close friendship?"

Nan was unflustered. "I know you're angry. You're trying to push away the people that care about you, that want to help you."

"Trust me, Andy did not want to help me. I'm not so sure he hasn't been framing me." It was out of her mouth before she could rein it back in. It was the thought that had been nagging her. Now it had finally found a voice right in front of Nan. She'd never leave now.

Charlie was right. Nan latched on to that morsel like a great white shark. "You think Andy is the murderer? And that he's setting you up to take the fall? "

Charlie tried to explain. "I know it sounds crazy, but after today I can't think of anything else that makes sense. Andy knew Kevin previously, they had a fight, and there was still bad blood between them. He never said a word about it to me, or Lance, for that matter. Then, I find out something today that ties everything together."

"What's that?" Nan asked.

"I'm sorry, Nan, I can't tell you," Charlie responded. "I'm going to have to figure this one out on my own."

"Please don't shut me out," Nan pleaded. "I'm your friend. Lance is your friend. He wants to help you. But you're going to have to stop hiding your past mistakes. Whatever you're trying to keep from him, he will find. That's his job, and he's very good at it. It would be so much easier if you worked with him and not against him."

Charlie knew Nan was just trying to help, but she didn't understand. "I have a right to my privacy. I don't want my past being dissected and gossiped about by people that don't even know me. I don't think that's too much to ask."

A shadow passed over Nan's face. "Yes. You have a right to your privacy. But what is so bad about your past that you can't share it with me?"

Charlie looked at Nan through tear-swollen eyes. "I told you that you didn't know me. I appreciate your visit, but I really just want to be alone right now."

Nan stood up. "Regardless of what you're feeling right now, you don't have to go through this by yourself. You have friends that love you and care for you. I'll let you have your solitude for the moment, but don't think that means I'm leaving you alone, not by a long shot."

Charlie walked Nan to the door. "Thanks for stopping by."

After Nan left, Charlie called Susan and told her she wouldn't be coming in for the rest of the day. She walked around the apartment, trying to organize the jumbled thoughts in her head. She finally settled on the couch in the sunroom, grabbed a cozy blanket, watched the hustle and bustle of small-town afternoon traffic, and thought of the evidence in Lance's folder. Nan was right. It was just a matter of time before Lance tracked down the whole story. He would find out that Charlie was at Kevin's trailer the night he was killed or find the gun and figure out it was hers. She was on borrowed time, and she still had so many unanswered questions.

Did she really think that Andy murdered Kevin? If Andy was telling the truth and both he and her grandmother had known her secret, then why had Betty

Ann never said anything? And how had Andy found out? He was the only one in Holiday Cove that could have provided Kevin with the information to blackmail her. Was he Kevin's partner? Maybe the fight between them was about more than a girl. If Kevin turned on Andy, then he would have had to take drastic measures. But why blackmail Charlie in the first place? What had she ever done to Andy to make him hate her? The morning's events had made Charlie tired, and the warm afternoon sunlight made her drowsy. She fell asleep with all the questions floating through her head. She had no idea how long she had been sleeping before Mr. Bear's sharp bark woke her. The setting sun told her it was longer than she usually would have slept. It was almost dinner time, her growling stomach reminded her.

She went into the kitchen to take care of Mr. Bear, but nothing looked appealing to her. She needed comfort food, but she refused to go out looking like this, and she had no desire to change. She picked up her phone and saw several messages from Nan and Susan. There was one from Andy begging her to talk to him. She didn't want to deal with any of them. Instead, she called in an order at the Chick-n-Hen. It would be about thirty minutes before the food arrived, so she decided to take a quick shower to wash the day away. After the shower, she changed into a pair of old sweatpants and a clean t-shirt. She had just put her hair up in a towel when the buzzer from the outside door sounded. She grabbed her wallet and opened the door. The familiar face of the auburn-haired waitress from the diner greeted her, but Charlie could never remember her name.

"You must think all I do is eat chicken," she said as she handed the girl a twenty.

The girl shrugged. "If you didn't, we wouldn't be in business." She tried to hand Charlie her change back, but Charlie waved her off.

"Keep it. It's worth every penny not step foot out of this apartment tonight."

"Thank you." The girl placed the extra cash in her pocket and handed Charlie the bag. "Enjoy."

Charlie thanked her again and shut the door. She took the food into the kitchen and wondered where Mr. Bear was. It wasn't like him to disappear. She found him hiding under the kitchen table.

"What are you doing under there, you silly boy?" She coaxed him out and gave him a treat. Whatever had spooked him was now forgotten.

Charlie inhaled the aroma of the greasy, fried food and poured herself a glass of tea. She wolfed down two pieces of fried chicken, mashed potatoes, and fried okra like she hadn't eaten in a month, then dug into the cherry pie. She had always been a stress eater. It was the main reason those extra twenty or so pounds were always hanging around. The overwhelming feeling of exhaustion returned. She cleaned up in the kitchen and went into the living room. She watched a little TV while her food digested and went to bed early. She'd try to figure out things in the morning. Maybe she would see things more clearly after a good night's sleep.

Fifteen

harlie's head felt like it was going to explode, and the banging on the door didn't help. She tried to sit up and realized she had fallen asleep on the couch again. Everything was fuzzy. She hadn't felt like this since she and Nan had gotten into some of Nan's father's moonshine. But she hadn't drunk a drop last night. All of the recent stress must have taken its toll on her. The banging on the outside entrance door continued.

"Charlie! Charlie! Open up right now!"

Charlie stumbled to the door.

"Lance! Quit yelling! I'm coming!"

She was still in her t-shirt and sweats from the night before, so she didn't bother to find her robe. But she was going to give Lance a piece of her mind for waking her up so early. The sun was barely up. She threw the door open.

"What do you want?" Charlie demanded.

"I need you to come with me." Charlie noticed the female officer standing behind him.

"No!" Charlie shouted. "I'm not answering any more of your questions. If you want to interrogate me more, you'll just have to arrest me."

Lance held up a pair of handcuffs. "Charlie Ann Flynn, you are under arrest for the murder of Kevin Wilson and the attempted murder of Andy Brock."

Charlie stared at him in shock. "Lance...."

"You have the right to remain silent. Anything you say can and will be used against you in a court of law. You have the right to talk to a lawyer and to have a lawyer present with you while you are being questioned. If you cannot afford to hire a lawyer, one will be appointed to represent you before any questioning if you wish. You can decide at any time to exercise these rights and not answer any questions or make any statements. Do you understand these rights?"

Charlie was confused. "You can't be serious. What's happened to Andy?"

Lance asked again. "Do you understand the rights I have just informed you of?"

It sunk in. The words echoed in her ears. Fate had chased her down, and Charlie resigned herself to its inevitable outcome.

"I understand," she whispered. "May I put on some shoes and call Susan to come to pick up Mr. Bear?"

Lance nodded and motioned for the female officer to follow Charlie.

"This is Officer Morgan. She'll be your shadow until we get back to the station. You have two minutes."

Charlie quickly called Susan. After she put on a pair of flip flops, she picked up Mr. Bear. She snuggled her face into his fur, trying not to cry.

"Susan's coming to pick you up. Everything's going to be fine. I'll be back. I promise." Mr. Bear wiggled from her grasp and licked her face. She had reached a new low, lying to a dog. She sighed as she put him in his kennel with a few of his toys. She turned to the young woman. "I'm ready."

The two of them walked back into the living room where Lance waited. He nodded to Officer Morgan, and she placed the cuffs on Charlie's wrists. Officer Morgan guided her down the steps and into the patrol car. Lance said nothing as they drove. Once they got to the station, Charlie was taken into a room that looked like a sterile lab.

Officer Morgan took the cuffs off and pointed to a rickety looking chair. "Have a seat over there and hold your hands out." She walked over to Charlie with a couple of swabs.

Charlie did as she was told and watched the young officer as she meticulously swabbed Charlie's fingers and hands. She then placed them in a bag and sealed them.

After dealing with the swabs, Officer Morgan handed Charlie a bag. "Stand up. I need you to remove your clothing and place them in here." Then she gave Charlie and ugly, tan jumpsuit. "You can put this on after you're finished."

Goosebumps broke out all over as her skin was exposed to the cold room. After she put her clothes in the bag, she hurriedly put on the jumpsuit. Once she was dressed, she was led to the same interrogation room she had been in the previous day. Charlie sat down at the wooden table. A tape recorder stared at her. She avoided looking at the two-way mirror. Finally, Lance walked in with two cups of coffee and the file from the day before. He placed the coffee in front of her.

"It's not bad for station coffee. I remember the way you like yours since Nan takes hers the same way."

Charlie didn't say anything as she reached for the cup. She wanted to refuse his act of kindness, but her head was still fuzzy, and she needed to be alert.

Lance turned on the tape machine. "For the record, Ms. Flynn, I have read you your rights, and you have refused an attorney at this time. Is that correct?"

"Yes."

He continued, "And you understand that you can stop questioning at any time and request an attorney?"

"Yes."

"Good. Then let's get started."

He handed her a piece of paper. "This warrant gives us permission to search your property, including the apartment, grounds, store, garage, and your vehicles."

"What happened to Andy?" Charlie asked.

"We'll get to that," Lance said.

Charlie stood her ground. "I'm not answering any of your questions unless you tell me what's happened to Andy, right now!" She tried to control the emotion in her voice but couldn't.

Lance placed his Stetson on the table and ran his fingers through his hair. "Are you telling me you don't know?"

Charlie wanted to smack the smug look off his face. "I've been trying to tell you all morning that I have no idea what's going on. But you're too pig-headed to listen to me!"

Lance leaned towards Charlie like he was going to tell her a juicy secret. "For the sake of speedin' all this up, I'll play along. Last night around ten, a woman walked into Andy's office and shot him. He'd be dead if someone didn't hear the shot and see the shooter run out the door."

Charlie felt sick. "And you think it was me?"

"Who else could I think it could be?" Lance sounded angry. "Half the town saw you arguing yesterday afternoon. I saw you fire him. And the witness said Andy was calling out your name."

Charlie was too stunned to speak.

Lance pushed the folder toward her. "And you had a motive," he said. "I told you I'd find out your secret. All I had yesterday was a picture and a name. Today, I have everything. Someone was kind enough to leave me the missing puzzle pieces this morning."

Charlie looked at the folder as if it was a snake poised to strike. She didn't need to open it. She knew what was in there.

Lance continued. "You found out that Andy knew everything too. He knew all about your troubles out there in California. Knew about your time in prison, knew about Jack Marsden, knew that you were an accused murderer. And then you figured the only way Kevin Wilson could have known all this about you was through Andy. You went to his office looking for the rest of the evidence. He came in and caught you. Then you did the only thing you could do. You shot him. Just like you shot Kevin."

Charlie shook her head. "I did figure out that Kevin got his information from Andy. But up until the moment you showed up at my door this morning, I thought Andy had killed Kevin and was trying to frame me for his murder."

"Now, why would he do that?" Lance asked.

"I don't know," Charlie tried to gather her thoughts. "I hadn't figured that part out yet."

"You thought one of your best friends was trying to frame you for murder, but you don't know why," Lance scratched his beard. "That just doesn't make a lick of sense to me."

"He was the only one who knew," Charlie whispered.

Lance opened the folder and pointed to the newspaper clippings. "It had to be hard on you, finding out that Andy knew your dirty little secret. I've seen your temper. You wouldn't let a betrayal like that pass."

Charlie finally looked down at the contents of the folder. Her twenty-two-year-old face stared back at her. Angry tears filled her eyes. "You think because I was accused of murder before that I must be your killer. Did you read the part where I was found innocent?"

Lance's face was stone cold. He kept tapping the folder. "I read the part where the jury was hung. I read the part where the county chose not to use their funds to re-try you. I read the part where your partner died in prison. I didn't read anything about you being innocent."

Charlie sat back in her chair for a moment and let the silence hang in the air between them. When she spoke again, she was composed, emotionless. "I've always questioned what it was about me that people could look at me and see me capable of taking a life. What kind of vibe do I give off? Are the words homicidal maniac written somewhere that only other people can see? Andy told me that my grandmother knew all of this too. I wonder what she thought. Did she wonder where she went wrong? Did I break her heart? I will tell you what I said to that detective all those years ago. There is nothing within me that would make me take a human life. I don't care what your evidence is. I don't care what you think. I don't care what you see. I am not a murderer."

Lance ignored her protest of innocence. "I've been mullin' things over, trying to figure out why Andy would sic a dog like Kevin Wilson on you. Here's what I think. Andy's had a thing for you all these years. You come back to town; he thinks maybe this time something will work out. Instead, you give him the "just friends" routine. He doesn't handle the rejection well. He has access to all these last-chancers at Ms. Lou's. He pays Kevin to send some not-so-nice letters. You're not dumb, you know you're gonna keep getting more of those letters until finally, someone puts a price tag on their silence. You can't let all of us judgmental yokels know you've been in prison on a murder charge. Once Kevin comes to your shop that day, you know he's your pen pal. Later on that night, you pay him a visit. And yes, we've found a witness that spotted your truck there. Whether you mean to or not, you shoot him. Later on, you find out his partner is none other than your good friend and lawyer. All the pieces fit. And if you were a better shot, Andy would be in the morgue, not the ICU."

A knock on the door interrupted Lance. Officer Morgan walked into the room and whispered in his ear. His expression told Charlie everything she needed to know.

"We found a gun and a black hoodie in your garage. We'll be runnin' some tests, but the caliber matches the evidence we have in both shootings.

Charlie closed her eyes. "I guess I'll be needing to call a lawyer now."

"Better get a good one," Lance said. "We're charging you with murder and attempted murder. Your bail hearing is this afternoon."

Sixteen

One of the good things about living in a small town is that there is virtually no crime, so Charlie had the jail cell all to herself. Lance had been generous with her phone privileges. She had been able to contact Susan, who recommended a lawyer, and Ms. Ada. She didn't know why she had contacted the latter, other than it gave her some kind of comfort to hear her voice. She had promised to be at her bail hearing. It was still a few hours away. Charlie tried to rest, but the firm mattress and antiseptic environment were not conducive to sleeping. Instead, she stared into space and wondered what she would do next. The test had come back positive for gun residue on her hands. They hadn't heard back from the lab yet on the clothing she had worn to the station or the hoodie they had found. She had a sinking suspicion they'd find her fingerprints on the gun as well.

Since Charlie didn't own a black hoodie, she knew it was a plant and more than likely had the damaging gunshot residue on it. She had been right that someone was framing her; she had just been wrong about who it was. She should have known it wasn't Andy. She suspected that growing up, he had a crush on her. But she hadn't wanted to be one of his many girlfriends. Even then, he wasn't the committing type. She had been surprised when she came back to town and found that he didn't have an active dating life. Instead, he had settled into the life of a confirmed bachelor. Now it appeared he was dating again and in spite of her best efforts, it bothered her. But that didn't matter anymore. He was fighting for his life and had named her the reason why. What had he seen to make him think she had shot him?

She was just too exhausted to think. She needed a shower and to brush her teeth. She had called the attorney that Susan had suggested, and she would be bringing her some clothes and personal items to freshen up with so she wouldn't go before the Judge in the horrible jumpsuit.

Charlie finally managed to rest until her lawyer arrived. Wren Kelly looked like she'd just finished high school instead of practicing law for over a decade. She had dated Susan's older brother, and even though the relationship hadn't worked out, she had stayed a close friend of the family. She didn't wear a stitch of make-up on her freckled face, and her sleek strawberry-blonde bob was held back with a tiny tortoiseshell headband. The gray suit she wore was perfectly tailored to fit her petite frame. She reached her hand out to shake Charlie's hand.

"They're giving us one of the conference rooms upstairs," Wren said. "It's got a small bathroom so you can freshen up while I order us some lunch. Gotta love that small-town hospitality. We'd be sitting in a cramped broom closet if we were in Nashville. Your bail hearing isn't for a couple of hours, so we have plenty of time. We'll get you out of that hideous jumpsuit and some food in your belly, and you'll feel human again."

Charlie liked Wren immediately. She felt comfortable with her fast talk and positive attitude. Officer Morgan led them to the conference room but stayed outside in the hallway. Charlie opened the overnight bag Susan had packed and sighed with relief. Everything she needed was in there.

"Where's a good place for lunch?" Wren asked.

"The Cool Cucumber is right across the street. Today's special should be black bean burgers and sweet potato fries."

"Sounds good to me, get changed, and I'll call in an order. Do they deliver?"

"They do," Charlie answered. "Have Jill put it on my tab and see if Officer Morgan wants anything."

Charlie left Wren to take care of the rest of the lunch details while she tried to make herself presentable. Her hair was a mess. She did her best to pick through the tangles before tying them into a loose bun at the nape of her neck.

She brushed her teeth and washed her face, applied some deodorant, and spritzed on some perfume. She didn't want to wear too much make-up, but she didn't want to look like warmed over death either. She applied a light layer of powder, then added some mascara and lipstick. Susan had picked out a simple navy maxi dress and matching flats. Charlie looked in the mirror. It wasn't something she would typically wear, but it was perfect for court. By the time she was ready, the food had arrived.

"I got us some organic lemonade too. I could drink this stuff by the gallon," Wren said.

Charlie agreed. "Jill is a magician in the kitchen."

The two women ate in silence for a few minutes before Wren handed Charlie some paperwork.

"While you finish eating, take a look at the contract. It's pretty standard. Usually, I would ask for ten percent up front. But I'm giving you the friends and family discount for Susan."

Charlie looked at her in disbelief.

"Don't be too surprised. I've seen that pink gold mine of yours. I'm not worried about getting paid. Plus, I trust Susan, and she says you're good for it."

Charlie asked the question she knew she shouldn't. "Aren't you worried about my guilt?"

Wren spoke matter-of-factly. "I don't ever worry about guilt or innocence. That's not my job. My job is to provide you the best defense possible. And that's what I'll do."

Charlie sighed. "I guess I just want somebody to believe I'm innocent."

Wren tried to be sympathetic. "Listen, every person that's ever been in your position has wanted that exact same thing. And I'll tell you what I told them. I don't care if anybody believes you're guilty or not except those twelve people on the jury. But our first step is to get you out on bail."

"Please," Charlie begged. "The last time, I couldn't afford bail. I had to spend months in prison, and I can't do that again."

"I'm not going to sugar coat it for you," Wren said. "They have a good case. They have GSR evidence, the gun, the jacket, and they'll fight to bring up your past. If you do get bail, can you swing it? "

Charlie nodded. "I have a little money left from my grandmother's estate. It should take care of it."

Wren looked at some more paperwork. "The other problem is they're going to say you're a flight risk. Give me something I can counteract that with."

"You've already said it, my pink gold mine. That house is all I have left of my grandmother. Holiday Cove is where I have chosen to make my home. I'm not leaving. I want my name cleared," Charlie said.

"I can work with that. Now, let's talk strategy and tell me everything about this other case in California."

Time flew by, and it wasn't long before Officer Morgan knocked on the door. It was time to head upstairs to the courtroom. It was out of her lips before she could stop it. "God, please don't make me go back to that jail cell."

"Amen," Wren whispered beside her.

Where had that come from? Charlie couldn't remember the last time she had uttered His name. She hadn't prayed once during the trial in California. It had only been a few words, but she had meant them. She would lose her mind if she had to spend any more time in that cell.

Charlie walked in the courtroom and saw Susan, Ms. Ada, and Brett sitting in the seats directly behind the defense table. Charlie's heart almost exploded at the sight of them. They all stood as Judge Marjorie Lewis walked in. Charlie recognized her from the store. She was an attractive older woman, probably in her late fifties. Her dark hair was pulled back in a severe bun that accentuated her hawk-like features, and her bright red lips off-set her stern black eyes. She was a fan of classic Chanel and had bought several pieces from Charlie. After everyone was sworn in and sat down, the hearing began.

Motions were made. Wren had been right about the State asking for no bail. District Attorney, Hoke Dodd, was a kindly looking, older gentleman. His thick hair was snow white, and Charlie had a feeling his southern drawl was played up for his audience. He reminded Charlie of a cross between Colonel Sanders and Matlock, one of her favorite TV lawyers.

"Ms. Flynn has only been a resident of Holiday Cove for less than a year. Before that, she spent her time traipsing around the country selling junk. There is nothing to prevent her from fleeing in the night and escaping the justice that is waiting for her. She is a flight risk, and we ask for no bail at this time."

Charlie had to force herself not to roll her eyes. This guy should have gone into the theater, not law. She looked at Wren. In this situation, her name fit her, she was a tiny bird about to be swallowed by a hungry tomcat. Wren walked in front of the defense table and smiled at the Judge.

"In spite of Mr. Dodd's poetic imagery of my client escaping her dire circumstance under the cloak of night, he could not be farther from the truth. Charlie Flynn has deep ties to this community. Her great-grandparents were one of its original settlers and her last remaining grandparent, Betty Ann Flynn recently passed away, leaving Charlie the family home. Instead of selling off her inheritance, she chose to restore the home, build a business, and make her life here. Everything she has is tied up in that house. She wants nothing more than to clear her name and get on with the life she has chosen here in Holiday Cove. We ask that Ms. Flynn be released on her own recognizance."

"Your Honor, if I may, I would ask for a moment of your time," Ms. Ada stood in the gallery.

Judge Lewis pursed her scarlet lips and squinted her eyes. "Ms. Ada, there is a protocol for these types of hearings."

"I understand, Judge, all I wanted to say was that I would stake my reputation that Charlie wouldn't leave. I would even volunteer as her guardian as long as she is here."

The Judge wrinkled her nose as if she smelled two-day old garbage. "Thank you, Ms. Ada, now please have a seat so I can rule on the subject at hand."

Ms. Ada sniffed and sat primly back down between Susan and Brett. Judge Lewis continued. "As much as I understand Mr. Dodd's impassioned plea, I don't think Ms. Flynn is a flight risk; however, the charges against her are severe. Bail will be set at a hundred thousand dollars, and the defendant will surrender her passport. And Ms. Ada, thank you for the generous offer of guardianship, but it will not be needed at this time. Ms. Flynn will be fitted with an ankle monitor that will let us know if she tries to leave the jurisdiction. With the upcoming July 4th holiday, we will reconvene on July 24th. Any objections? " The lawyers consulted their calendars and agreed on the trial start date. "Court is adjourned!" The gavel banged Charlie's freedom.

She shook Wren's hand and hugged her friends. "Thank you all for being here. Please come by the apartment this evening for dinner. I don't want to be alone."

They all agreed. Susan hugged Charlie again. "I'm going back to the store. Your arrest hasn't slowed down business. We're slammed! Let me know when you get up to the apartment, and I'll bring Mr. Bear up. He's missed you, and I know you've missed him."

"Thank you, Susan. I don't know what I would do without you."

Susan smiled. "I promise you aren't going to have to find out."

As the courtroom emptied, Charlie turned back to Wren. "When do we get started planning my defense?"

"Right now," Wren said. "Susan's offered up her guest bedroom for the duration. I just need some workspace."

"Use the office in my apartment. Let me know what you need, and I'll get it for you."

Wren nodded. "It looks like we have a plan, let's get started."

Seventeen

Even though Susan said the shop had been busy, Charlie wasn't prepared for the sight of all the cars around the pink Victorian, especially so near closing time. Luckily, she managed to sneak into the garage and up the back entrance before being spotted. After paying bail and getting fitted for her ankle monitor, all Charlie wanted to do was get home. She was thankful not to be under house arrest. The beacon allowed her to go as far as the county line before going off.

Wren had driven over to Susan's house to drop off her things and would be back for dinner that night. Charlie had wanted to go see Andy, but Wren nixed the idea. He was still in ICU, in a coma. If and when he woke up, they didn't know what he would say. Wren thought it best for Charlie to keep her distance until they knew more. As hard as it was, Charlie agreed. She'd stopped at the Cool Cucumber and picked up a couple of white pizzas for her dinner guests. She was more than a little nervous walking in after everything that had happened, but both Jill and Tony had treated her kindly, offering her prayers and encouragement. There were some stares and hostile looks from a few others in the store, but it was from faces she didn't recognize, and thankfully, no one made a scene. She had about an hour before her friends arrived and debated between a shower or a nap. A quick sniff vetoed the nap. She showered and changed into a weathered pair of Levi's and a plain white tee. Tonight was informal, and she just wanted to be comfortable. She left her wet hair down to air dry and didn't bother with putting on any shoes or socks. She went around the apartment, lighting candles, and found a good jazz station to play quietly in the background. She was doing everything she could to relax. She had never felt more thankful for her home. She could have been spending the night alone in a cold jail cell rather than here with her friends. She hadn't forgotten about her prayer or the answer it seemed to have gotten. But right now, she couldn't wrap her head around much more than putting the pizzas in the oven. She also bought some fresh strawberries and whip cream to top one of Jill's angel food cakes. A little after five, she heard a scratch at the interior apartment entrance and a smile spread across her face. She opened the door, and Mr. Bear bounded in followed by Susan.

"My little buddy!" Charlie knelt on the floor and scooped her furry companion into her arms. "I got you a special treat because I know what a good boy you've been today. I missed you so much!" She squeezed him until he grunted to be let down.

"Susan, I can't thank you enough for watching him. If anything had happened..."

Susan gave her friend a hug. "Everything's okay."

Charlie took a deep breath. "What's in the bag?"

Susan pulled out a six-pack of Cheerwine. "I thought you might like a treat."

She took the drinks from Susan and headed into the kitchen. Charlie did her best to stay away from soda, but every now and then she would allow herself a bottle. Cheerwine had always been a childhood favorite. Her grandmother always kept the fridge stocked with them when she came to visit. It was sweet that Susan remembered something from one of her numerous childhood stories.

"The pizza should be done in a few minutes. Let me get Mr. Bear his promised treat, and I'll set the table." She went to the pantry and led the pooch to his kennel. "Look what I found. This will keep you occupied for a while." Charlie handed him a pig ear like the one he'd had at Ms. Lou's. He could snack while she and the others had dinner. She went back to the kitchen, washed her hands, and started setting the table. The smell of the pizza mingled with the lemon-scented candles and the apartment began to smell like an Italian restaurant. After Brett, Ms. Ada, and Wren arrived, they all sat down to dinner. The conversation was casual through dessert until they moved into the living room. The setting sun and warm coffee invoked a calming environment. Ms. Ada was the first to speak up. She looked like an ancient queen in her deep amethyst kaftan with matching head wrap and large gold hoops dangling from her ears.

"Dear, we know that today was trying for you and the next few weeks are going to be even more difficult. We just want you to know that we're here for you."

Charlie nodded. She honestly had the best friends. She tried not to think of Nan and Andy not sitting here in this room with the everyone else, but in her heart, she knew their absence was unavoidable.

Charlie stared at the floor and began to speak softly. She couldn't look them in the eyes, but she wanted them to know what she was really up against. In her mind, these next few weeks were just to say goodbye. There was no defense against the evidence they had, and once her past came to light, whatever community support she had would be gone.

"Wren heard this story today, and we are both sure that the district attorney will somehow manage to make sure everyone in the courthouse hears it as well. They think it's my motive for murdering Kevin and shooting Andy. I've tried to keep this part of my life secret, but Kevin found out about and began sending me letters. We all believe he planned on blackmailing me. Because of my suspicions that

Kevin got this information from Andy, the DA believes I killed Kevin to prevent him from blackmailing me and shot Andy because I found out about his part in the scheme. I'm ashamed that I ever thought Andy could be capable of something so heinous. Before my sins go on display for the whole town to see, I wanted to tell you, my friends, first. I understand that after this, you might feel differently about me. In all honesty, I can't say I would blame you."

Charlie lifted her eyes. "When I went to college in California, I fell in love with an older man. He was a local businessman that was heavily involved in the arts program at our school. I met him at one of the gallery openings and developed a crush. The feelings were reciprocated, and we began seeing each other. He treated me like an adult. We went to plays and operas, fancy dinners, expensive weekend getaways. We had been seeing each other for almost six months when he finally told me that he was married. I should have ended it right then and there, but I didn't. Instead, we continued to see each other for the next three years. He paid for my apartment, my car, anything I wanted or needed. I knew what I was doing was wrong, but I didn't care. I tried not to think about his wife or his life with her.

"I was a good student and kept my grades up. I excelled in my classes and was set to graduate with honors. An art gallery out of Rome had just made a significant acquisition of early Greco-Roman pieces and had interviewed me for an intern position since that era had been the focus of my studies. The internship would be for two years. It came with a small stipend and free room and board. It was an offer I couldn't pass up. When I told Jack I accepted the position, he was furious, and we argued the whole night. Even though I loved him, I wanted more than to be his mistress. I told him I was going to Rome with or without him. I gave him an ultimatum that if he wanted to go with me, he had to leave his wife and start a new life in Rome with me. He said he'd work things out.

"The next two weeks things were tense but normal. I was studying for finals and getting ready for graduation. One day, the police came to my door. Jack had been arrested for murdering his wife but claimed I was responsible. He planted evidence that made it look like I had been involved in the planning of her murder. He said that I had been jealous and angry that he wouldn't go to Italy with me. The police believed we were both involved. There was enough false evidence planted by Jack that they believed I helped him. He maintained his innocence and blamed everything on me.

"They set our trial dates separately. He got out on bail. No one would believe that I had nothing to do with it. My bail was set at half a million dollars. I had no money, and I couldn't tell my grandmother, so I had to spend almost three months in prison. I was fortunate that my court-appointed attorney was good at his job. He was able to cause enough doubt about the evidence that the jury hung.

"Jack's trial didn't go well for him. He was found guilty and sentenced to life in prison. His motive was strong. Most of the assets and money came from his wife. If he wanted to start a life in Rome with me, he'd have to leave all that behind, plus he had a substantial life insurance policy on her. And the evidence against him was good. He'd tried to make the murder look like an accident, but he'd been sloppy. Blaming me had been his plan B. With no new evidence on me, and Jack's guilty verdict, the DA decided not to burden the State with the expense of another trial for me, and the charges were dropped. But it didn't matter, by that time my life was in shambles. My college expelled me for my conduct, the invitation for the internship was rescinded, and I was broke. But more than that, I couldn't escape the shame and guilt I felt. I had knowingly carried on that affair. I might not have known the path that Jack would take, but I knew there could be consequences to my actions. Whether I killed her or not, her blood is on my hands, and I live with that every day."

The room was silent for a few minutes. Ms. Ada moved from the couch and knelt in front of Charlie's chair.

"Sweet girl, what a burden you have carried all these years. My heart aches for you. You made a bad choice in a man. But his actions and his actions alone are responsible for his wife's death, not yours. You have been so afraid to share this with others, and it's kept you isolated. This hasn't changed how I feel about you in any way. And I know Betty Ann would have felt the same way."

At the mention of her grandmother's name, Charlie finally broke down. The years of hiding, the shame, the guilt, all of the events of the past few days finally overtook her. Sobs racked her body, and the tears flowed freely. She could hear Betty Ann's voice in her head.

"It's time to stop running. God isn't done with you yet."

Eighteen

After the breakdown, her friends had rallied around her. Her greatest fear had not come to fruition. Her friends had not abandoned her when they heard about her past. Instead, they had embraced her. They stayed until way past midnight, offering words of encouragement. By the time everyone left, she felt calmer. The tears had been cathartic. Now she sat alone in the darkness, the candlelight casting shadows on the wall. She looked through the window into the courtyard of the old church next door. Since moving in upstairs, she had seen many people come to the little garden to pray. Its welcoming fountain and carefully tended greenery invited quiet reflection.

The church made her think of her parents and how they had given their lives to serve God. They had attended several different churches during her father's time as Chaplain. Some of them were grand with thousands of members, while others were small country chapels with only a handful of parishioners. Charlie felt empty in all of them.

She knew her grandmother thought the death of her parents had caused her crisis of faith. But the truth was there had never been a crisis of faith because she had never had any to begin with. In her heart, she had never believed. Any act of contrition had been for her parents benefit. After they had gone, she let herself retreat further into her doubt. What kind of God took a girl's family when she needed the most? However, something in that desperate plea not to go back to jail had been real. Somehow, a long-buried part of her still believed. She had heard the stories of forgiveness, of redemption and could even recite them from memory. They were in her head but had never made it to her heart. Being confronted with her past had left her questioning. She wanted to heed her grandmother's advice and stop running. But she didn't know if she could. She remembered the confinement, the fear, the hopelessness of prison. She didn't want to go back. She could run, but she would never be free. This was where she had to make her stand.

She needed for Andy to wake up, for a lot of reasons. She needed to talk to him and wanted him to be okay. She had to find out why he thought she shot him. But since she couldn't speak to him, she'd start with the guy at the motel where Kevin Wilson first made his appearance in Holiday Cove. Wren would be here early in the morning, and they would go to the motel together. They had also decided that Susan would take over the day-to-day operations of running the store. Charlie didn't want her life turned into a circus if she could avoid it, and it would give her more time to help Wren with her defense.

Finally, her thoughts stopped racing, and drowsiness began to overtake her. She had never been more thankful for her bed than she was that night. She crawled in under the soft covers and fell fast asleep.

*

The next morning Wren and Susan showed up with coffee and croissants. Wren looked even more like a teenager in her jeans and Vandy law t-shirt.

"You might get run out of town for your outfit choice this morning. Didn't Susan tell you that you were in Big Orange country?"

Wren laughed. "I'm a big girl, and I'm sure I can handle any disgruntled fans. Where do you want to start this morning?"

"At the beginning or what we know to be the beginning, the Holiday Motor Lodge. A man named Jonas Wells remembers Kevin and his girlfriend, and I can't help but think that she's the key."

"I saw in the files where he was supposed to give a description to a sketch artist at the police station, but there was no sketch," Wren said.

"I wonder if he ever made it to the station," Charlie replied. "If not, maybe we can get him to talk to us. I'm no

Monet, but I can draw a little if he would give us a description of her."

Susan took a sip of her coffee. "Sounds like you two have your day planned, what do you need from the gang and me downstairs?"

"How are we on inventory?" Charlie asked.

"We're going to need a restock by the weekend. Friday's Lunch on the Lawn will have us hopping."

The tourists would be coming into town by the droves starting Thursday night, and the store would probably get some early bird traffic that day, but by Friday the streets and sidewalks would be jam-packed with out- of- towners. Lunch on the Lawn officially kicked off the July 4th festivities. The mayor and his staff grilled hamburgers and hot dogs for the whole community. The winner of the best-decorated store would be announced as well. People picnicked on the Courthouse lawn and explored the downtown shops, and Charlie wanted the store to be full.

"After we get back from the motor lodge, I'll run to the storage unit. Make a list of where we're bare, and I'll restock tonight after everyone's gone home. Do you think it's too busy for Mr. Bear to be downstairs? I can take him to doggy daycare before I leave."

"Oh, no! Customers love him. Plus, the girls take their breaks with him. They'd mutiny if I don't bring him downstairs."

Charlie laughed. "We can't afford a mutiny on our hands. Better take him then."

She grabbed a red, white, and blue bow tie then gave Mr. Bear a kiss on his wet nose before handing Mr. Bear off to Susan. "You be a good boy for Susan and the girls, and we'll take a ride when we get back."

The dog's ears perked up at one of his favorite words. Charlie scratched his chin and then gave Susan his leash. "Call me if you need anything."

"I will. You two try and stay out of trouble."

"No promises," Wren said.

Charlie left Wren to her coffee while she did a quick change into a pair of red denim shorts with a blue and white horizontal stripe sleeveless blouse that tied behind her neck. She tied her hair up in a ponytail and fastened it with a bright red, white, and blue scarf. White sunglasses and navy Keds completed her patriotic look.

"Do you want to take my car or yours?" Charlie asked as she walked back into the kitchen.

"Let's take mine. I want to try her out on these curvy country roads."

Wren's bright yellow Audi Cabriolet convertible suited her perfectly. She pulled a baseball cap from the glove compartment and put on her sunglasses.

"This was a little gift to myself after my fiancé dumped me two days before our Christmas wedding. I think I came out ahead. Don't you?"

Charlie ran her fingers over the leather as she got into the car. "I sure do!"

Wren smiled. "All right then, let's go see if we can find this mystery woman."

Nineteen

Charlie loosened her grip on the door handle as Wren found a parking space at the Holiday Motor Lodge.

"Do you think you might have missed your calling as a race car driver?" Charlie asked.

"What? Did I scare you?" Wren teased.

"Oh, no," Charlie answered. "I always look this shade of green."

Wren laughed. "Sorry, I'll drive slower going back."

"Good! The last thing I need is my lawyer in jail for reckless endangerment."

"Okay, okay!" Wren threw her hands up in surrender. "I get your point. Now let's go see what this guy remembers."

Jonas Wells was a charming little man that spoke with a deep southern accent. Time had lost him somewhere in the seventies. His jet-black hair most definitely came from a bottle and was slicked back with enough gel and hairspray that not one hair moved. His bright green polyester shirt was tucked into a too-big pair of avocado pants made of the same material. A thick brown belt struggled to hold them up, and a large gold watch hung loosely from a thin, tanned wrist.

"Good morning ladies, the name's Jonas Wells. I do apologize, but check-in isn't until three." He spoke every word with a slow drawl.

"Oh, we're not checking in, sir. We just need a little information, and we hear in these parts you're the man to ask." Wren smiled as she put on the charm.

Jonas smiled back and showed a mouth full of pearly whites that probably cost more than Charlie's first car. He smoothed down his shirt and adjusted his amber-tinted glasses.

"Well, miss, just what kind of information are y'all looking for? This ain't the Welcome Center, ya know!"

"Of course, you're not!" Wren put a hundred-dollar bill on the counter. "Please, let me introduce myself. My name's Wren, and this here is Charlie. We're trying to find a friend of ours that stayed here sometime before Christmas. And then he just up and disappeared. He was supposed to meet us in Atlanta after New Year's, but he never showed up, and we've been looking everywhere for him. So we decided to take the trip up from Georgia ourselves to see you. I just know you'll be able to help us."

Charlie vowed never to underestimate Wren again. She could Jonas eyeing the bill. He quickly put his hand over it and slipped into his back pocket.

"Well, I guess I can spare a few minutes, but I got plenty to do before the check-in rush. Come on back to my office. What did ya say your friend's name was?"

"Kevin Wilson," Wren said.

The girls followed the little man to a cramped office that had been decorated in early Brady Brunch. He moved stacks of papers and folders off two bright orange chairs and then sat down behind a desk so big his feet didn't touch the ground. He reached into one of the drawers and brought out a bag of pork rinds, and started munching.

"I'm sorry. I'm being rude, would y'all like any?" He offered them the bag. Both girls shook their heads, and he shrugged. "I used to weigh over three-hundred pounds. Then I started hearin' bout how eatin' low carbs can help ya lose weight. I got pork rinds and Slim Jims hid all over the place in case I get the munchies. And let me tell ya, it works. I lost over a hundred and fifty pounds! You girls sure you don't want some? I mean, I ain't sayin' you need to lose weight or anything. I just don't want y'all to be hungry."

Charlie could see they were getting off track. "You sure look great! I'm glad the diet's working for you, but we ate before we came. We're just so thankful for you helping us find Kevin."

Jonas put the bag down and folded his hands on the desk. He sighed deeply. "I do hate to be the one to tell you, but he's dead. Murdered."

Wren clasped her hand to her chest. "Gracious! Do you know what happened?"

Jonas shook his head. "I don't go to town much. The Wal-Mart is right across the road, and that has everything I need. I don't like to be away from the place long, you see. But you should go see Lance Holiday, he's the one working the case. Came out here not two days ago, asking all kinds of questions."

"Please, can you tell us what you told him?" Charlie asked.

Jonas crunched on a pork rind. "As you can see, I run a respectable establishment."

The girls nodded. Even though the old motel looked like it hadn't been updated since the sixties, everything was clean, flowers bloomed around the entrance, and the area was quiet.

"I don't cotton to no riff-raff, and I don't put up with no shenanigans. Your friend did come in right before Christmas. Had a gal with him. They paid for a couple nights. I hate to say it, but I had a feeling they might be up to no good. But it was almost Christmas, and well, I always think about Mary and

Joseph and how some cranky old' innkeeper left them out in the cold, so I try to be extra accommodating around that time of year. The second night they were here, they went to howlin' at each other. Had to be after midnight. All my rooms were full on account of everyone travelin' for the holidays so I couldn't afford them causing a ruckus. I went out to their room and knocked on the door. The boy opened the door, and I told him they better straighten up or get out. He promised they'd behave. Didn't hear nothin' else from him until the next morning. That girl had done left him high and dry. Took the car, took the money, she even took every stitch of clothes, 'cept the ones he was wearin'. I might have let him stay a night or two out of kindness, but when I went to check the room, they had trashed it. Empty beer and liquor bottles, cigarette butts everywhere, and I ain't so sure I didn't smell some weed. I let my temper get the best of me. Told him if he didn't get off my property, I'd call the law. I guess he walked all the way into town."

Wren leaned forward. "What about the girl? Do you remember what she looked like?"

Jonas closed his eyes like he was trying to concentrate. "I didn't get a real good look at her. I was s'posed to go down to the police station and talk to one of those art fellas, but I just ain't got 'round to it yet."

"I'm a bit of an artist myself," Charlie said. "Do you think you could describe her to me?" She took the sketch pad and pencil out of her purse.

"I'll sure try," he said. "I sure would like to help you nice girls. I'd say she was about average height, would fit right perfect between the two of y'all. Had long, stringy dark blonde hair, come almost all the way down her back. Thin.

Couldn't tell ya what color her eyes were but they was just sad, you know what I mean? They had some bags under 'em like she hadn't slept much. Real pasty skin. Her cheeks were kind of sunk in. Made it look like those girls that make that silly face when they pucker their lips. 'Cept she wasn't puckerin' hers. Real stern lookin' like her face would crack if she tried to smile. She was probably closer to your age than your friend's."

Charlie tried to draw as fast as Jonas talked. When she was done, she showed him the picture. "Is this close?"

He scratched his head and stared at it. "Pretty close. Her nose was longer and a little thinner. You got her eyes right. Dead."

Charlie made the adjustment to the nose and showed him the picture again. "That's her. Say! You sure can draw good."

Charlie smiled. "Is there anything else you can think of? Did she ever come back, or have you seen her again?"

"Ya know, now that you mention it, I coulda swore I seen her at the Wal-Mart the other day, 'cept it wasn't entirely like she was the same."

Wren and Charlie exchanged a look.

"Do you mean she changed her appearance?" Wren asked.

The man looked confused. "I'm sorry. It's hard to explain. I just caught a glimpse of her. I don't know if it was the way she moved or what she was wearing. It was just a split second, ya know? Like my brain didn't register I even seen her 'til just now when you asked about it."

Charlie nodded. "Mr. Wells, you've been a great help. Thank you."

"Anytime. Like I said, y'all go talk to that friendly officer. I'm sure he'd know more than me."

They waved to Jonas as they got into the little car.

"Charlie, that girl is still in town. If we find her, we might be able to get to the bottom of this!" Wren was excited.

Charlie agreed. But just how were they going to find the girl?

Twenty

After the girls got back to Charlie's apartment, Wren went to her temporary office and Charlie went to the storage locker with the list Susan had given her. By the time she got back, Susan had closed up the store, and everyone was gone. After a quick bite to eat, she and Mr. Bear went downstairs to start work. She pulled the truck up to the back entrance of the store and began unloading boxes. As she was coming out the back door, Nan's black SUV pulled into the driveway.

"You shouldn't be here, Nan. I don't want to talk to you."

Charlie's warning didn't deter her friend. "And I believe I told you that you weren't going through this without me. I came by the store today, and Susan said you'd be restocking inventory tonight. I thought I could lend a hand, plus I don't like the thought of you being alone. Come on, Charlie. I even wore work clothes."

Charlie shook her head. Only Nan would think work clothes consisted of designer jeans and high heels. Charlie walked back inside and then turned around. "You're going to wish you wore a different pair of shoes by the end of the night."

Nan grinned and grabbed a box. They worked hard restocking shelves and tables. Charlie couldn't believe how much inventory had been sold. Susan deserved a raise, and if Charlie made it through this, she'd make sure she got one. The thought of losing this place almost brought her to tears. The bail money had wiped out her cash reserve. She had less than one hundred dollars in her checking account, nothing in her savings, and a thousand-dollar CD she'd pay some hefty penalties on if she had to use it. She had to put the Victorian up as collateral for the bail. The only bright spot was that Wren had waived her fee. Charlie had tried to argue, but Wren was stubborn. She refused to let Charlie wipe out her savings and said she could afford to handle the case pro bono.

Charlie brought the box she was carrying into the main showroom where Nan was sorting through a collection of vintage postcards. Charlie felt a chill walking into the room. So much had happened in the short time since the confrontation with Kevin. Charlie walked over to the knife case. She tried to remember life before that moment.

"Hey!" Nan's voice interrupted her thoughts. "I think we need a coffee break."

Charlie looked at the time. They had been working for almost two hours straight. "You're right! I may even be able to find some stale biscotti."

Nan laughed. "Who can resist stale biscotti?"

Charlie started the coffee and found Mr. Bear a treat. He curled up at Charlie's feet while she and Nan talked.

"Does Lance know you're here?" Charlie asked.

Nan nodded. "I left him a note. Let's just say we're not exactly on speaking terms."

"Because of me?" Charlie asked.

"Not because of you, because of him," Nan said. "I don't understand how he can believe you had anything to do with any of this, especially shooting Andy. I was out of town on a buying trip when he arrested you, and he didn't even call to tell me. You didn't call me either, so I had no idea what was happening until I got home this morning. Do you really think I wouldn't have dropped everything to be there for you?" Tears began to roll down Nan's face. "You act like we're strangers, but you forget that I know the real you. I was the first person you told that you were afraid of the dark. I spent a whole weekend at your house eating mint chocolate chip ice cream with you when Seth Anderson broke your heart the summer before high school. I never left your side while you mourned for your parents. I was there for you when you buried Betty Ann. And then I find out you've kept this secret from me."

"How did you find out?" Charlie asked.

"Lance left your file in his office at the house," Nan said. "I know I shouldn't have read it, but I did. Why didn't you tell me? Even if you couldn't have told me then, why not now? Did you really think it would change anything between us? You're my best friend, and I love you!"

Charlie reached for Nan's hand.

"I couldn't tell anyone. I was so naive. I thought being innocent meant something, but it didn't. You have no idea what prison is like. I couldn't let anyone see me like that. My lawyer was good, and the evidence was flimsy. I should have been found not guilty. After the fact, we found out most of the jury believed the evidence was insufficient. But there was a couple of jurors that felt because of the affair, I had to have played some part in the murder. I didn't say anything later because it was a part of my life that I just wanted to forget. I knew if people found out about my past, I would always be on trial. And there would be those that no matter what the evidence said, would find me guilty. I'd be labeled a home wrecker, a murderer, and whatever other labels could be thrown at me. I wasn't going to live the rest of my life like that."

Nan squeezed Charlie's hand. "Sweetie, everyone has made a mistake in their life. No one has any right to judge you. I most certainly don't. But it seems to me, you're the one that keeps finding yourself guilty. Not all prisons have bars and locks."

Charlie sighed. "Ms. Ada and I talked about this last night. She says I need to forgive myself."

"Ms. Ada is a wise woman. You should listen to her. Or, have you thought of talking to Pastor Richard? Betty Ann thought highly of him. See if you can get rid of some of this baggage you carry around. He is only right next door, after all."

Charlie shrugged her shoulders. "Maybe."

Nan sensed Charlie's discomfort and switched subjects. "For what it's worth, I think Andy was trying to do the right thing by not telling you that he knew about your past."

"You may be right, but it just bothers me that he's known all this time and never said anything. Of course, it could also explain why he's never asked me out. Having an accused murderer as your girlfriend could be tough for a lawyer."

Nan playfully slapped Charlie's arm. "Now you're just being silly. That man has been in love with you all his life."

Charlie shook her head. "We'd never work. Some people are just meant to be friends."

Nan rolled her eyes. "You two could be poster children for the whole "love is blind" thing."

A knock on the door interrupted their laughter. Charlie answered the door then walked back into the kitchen with Lance following behind her.

"Lance, what are you doing here? I don't want to talk; I'm helping Charlie with her inventory."

Lance looked at his wife.

"We'll talk later, but right now, I need Charlie to come with me. Andy just woke up, and he wants to see Charlie."

Twenty-One

Charlie and Nan followed Lance down the long hallway. The couple hadn't spoken a word on the car ride over. Charlie felt a twinge of guilt that her circumstances were causing problems in her friend's marriage. Lance finally stopped walking when he reached the room at the end of the hall.

"He wants to speak to you alone. We'll wait out here."

Charlie entered the room and was surprised to see Andy sitting up and eating.

Charlie tried to keep the mood light. "If I had known you were able to eat, I would have snuck you in a burger."

Andy looked up from his tray. "Hey, Charlie. Glad you could make it. Come sit down."

She couldn't read his face. The pain he was in was masking any emotion he might be feeling. She sat in the chair beside his bed and waited for him to speak.

"I talked to Lance," he said. "I tried to clear things up, but I don't know if I did any good. I don't know what I said or what the guy that found me heard, but I wasn't naming you my shooter."

Charlie moved her chair closer to him. "It doesn't matter. I'm just glad to see you're okay. You had me scared!"

Andy looked at her. "My Moll scared? I don't buy it for a minute."

For the first time, his stupid nickname for her didn't make her cringe. "You can think whatever you want, I've been a mess. I just wish I could have come sooner. And what about Gus? Was he hurt?"

"Nah, I'd left him at the farm," Andy said. "Ms. Lou's going to watch him for me until I can go home."

"That's a relief. You know if you need anything...." The words hung in the air.

"I know," he said. "We'll make it through this."

"Andy, I'm so sorry." Tears brimmed in Charlie's eyes. "All I have been able to think about is all the terrible things I said to you. I should never even have thought them, let alone yelled them at you across the courthouse lawn. Now, Lance and the DA think you have something to do with Kevin. Everything's a mess, and it's all my fault."

Andy handed her a tissue. "Charlie, I'm not angry with you. You've spent your life trying to hide from this thing. I didn't tell your grandmother about your trouble in California, she told me. That creep, Jack Marsden, sent her a letter after your trial with all the clippings and photos. He made threats that he would get to you, get his revenge. That's why she never pressured you about settling down here. She thought you'd be safer on the road. When she got sick, she showed me everything because she knew she was dying. She didn't know whether leaving you the Victorian would be a good idea or not. She was afraid Jack would find you and carry out his threat. I looked into some things for her and found out he was dead. He died in an escape attempt almost two months before. We felt like there was no threat, but she wanted me to hang on to the letter and the clippings just in case. They're still in my safety deposit box at the bank. I had nothing to do with blackmailing you. I could never do anything to bring you harm. Lance can investigate me all he wants; he's not going to find any evidence against me."

Charlie regained her composure. "I guess this is why people shouldn't keep secrets. If I had just told her, maybe some of this trouble could have been avoided. I wish I had known Jack was tormenting her. She didn't deserve that. I never told anyone this, but I went to see Jack about a year after he'd been sent to prison. He'd sent a letter to me through my lawyer. When I got there, he made some veiled threats. He blamed me for everything, he said I had no loyalty. He truly believed I should have been satisfied living out the rest of my life as his mistress. He said since I ruined his life, that he would ruin mine. He promised to make sure that I was never happy or never safe, and I believed him. I thought I was protecting my grandmother by staying away. My lawyer sent me a letter when Jack died. That's why I felt safe enough to stay here and try to start a life. I thought I was free, but I'm not. Someone's trying to send me back to prison. And everyone thinks I shot you!"

Andy touched her face. "I would know you in the dark with a blindfold on. It wasn't you in the office that night, and I'll do whatever it takes to help you prove that."

Charlie blushed like she was in junior high again. "I'm just glad whoever it was didn't kill you."

"That's the strange thing," Andy said. "I don't think they were trying to. That or they were a horrible shot. Doc said the bullet went straight through and missed any major arteries or organs by a mile. The problem was I lost too much blood. This new medicine I've been taking thinned it out too much. I should be fine in a couple of days. I might even get out of here by the Stars and Stripes Gala."

The fanciest event for the holiday festivities was the Stars and Stripes Gala hosted by Lance's parents at the Holiday mansion. It was a formal occasion, and almost everyone in town would be there dressed in their red, white, and blue best.

"I think Holiday Cove's most eligible bachelor is going to need to sit this one out," Charlie said. "You're in no shape to be going anywhere."

"And disappoint all my fans? Now Charlie, you know I can't do that," Andy quipped.

"Speaking of adoring fans, are you going to tell me about the girl you and Kevin were arguing about?" Charlie asked.

"Yes, but it's not what you think," Andy answered. "I was seeing Lila from the Chick-N-Hen, but we weren't serious. She was there the day Kevin, and I fought, but she wasn't who we were arguing about. You were. I'd heard him questioning one of the other guys about you. After Lila left, I confronted him about it. He said some very un-gentleman like things, and I told him to stay away from you. He told me to mind my own business, and I explained to him that you were my business. He just wouldn't shut up, and I wasn't going to let him keep talking about you like that. I'm not proud, but I won't say I wouldn't do it again. The reason I didn't say anything once I found out about the blackmail and Kevin's obsession with you was that I thought it would make you look more guilty. I guess I was trying to protect you."

Charlie took a moment to process what he had said. She ignored the resurgence of butterflies and concentrated on the facts.

"You're saying Kevin knew about me before he worked for Brett. How? And how did he know so much about my past?"

Andy shrugged. "That's what I've been trying to find out. I've re-read all my notes and files from your case in California. I can't find anyone still alive with a link to Kevin. It's like he pulled your name out of a hat and decided to torture you."

"I don't believe in coincidence," Charlie said. "Wren and I got a description of the girl that abandoned him from Jonas today. I think she has something to do with all this."

"Who's Wren?"

"My lawyer. She's a friend of Susan's."

"Are you going to fire her now that I'm back on the case?" Andy asked.

Charlie shook her head. "You're not back on the case. You got too close to something that someone didn't want you to know. I want you to stay out of it. Anyway, I need you more as my friend than my lawyer."

"I'll let you fire me as your lawyer," Andy said. "But if you think I'm staying out of this, you're gonna be disappointed. I'm in this with you. I'm not letting you go back to prison."

Charlie smiled. "For now, please just get some rest. I'll come back in the morning and sneak you in some donuts."

"Chocolate. With sprinkles. Lots of sprinkles."

"Deal! I'll see you in the morning." Charlie squeezed his hand and stood up. Somehow her feet felt lighter as she walked out the door.

Twenty-Two

After a good night's sleep, Charlie woke up early, ate breakfast, took Mr. Bear for a walk, and cleaned the apartment. Then she talked to Wren and Susan about staying out of the shop. With Lunch on the Lawn happening that afternoon, all hands would be needed in the store and Charlie was tired of hiding. This was her life, and she was going to fight for it.

She had just finished tidying the living room when she saw Pastor Richard enter the church next door. The store didn't open for another hour, so she had time to see him. She hoped he wasn't busy. She quickly put on a full red skirt, white button up blouse, and patent navy flats with a matching belt. She had pin rolled her hair last night, and now her locks fell in perfect red curls around her shoulders. She tied, a red, white, and blue scarf around her neck, and found a pair of earrings to match. She put Mr. Bear in his kennel and walked through her backyard to the front entrance of the church.

It was one of the oldest churches in Holiday Cove, a dark stone building with a majestic white steeple. Charlie had always loved the large red oak door. A wreath of fresh, red and white carnations with a large blue ribbon hung in the center. She opened the door and started down the long hallway that led to the sanctuary. A small sign with an arrow pointed Charlie to the church office down another hall. A jovial brunette with a pageboy haircut greeted Charlie from behind a sparse wooden desk.

"Good morning, I'm Ruth, how can I help you?"

"Hi, Ruth. My name's Charlie Flynn, I live next door. I don't have an appointment, but I was hoping to speak to Pastor Richard."

"Of course. He's usually off on Friday, but he likes being here during big events in case someone needs him. I think he just stepped out to water the flowers in the garden. Would you like to wait for him?"

Charlie shook her head. "If it's okay, I'll just go to the garden."

"Sure thing," Ruth said. "Take the exit door to the right in the sanctuary, and it will take you there."

"Thank you." Charlie wondered how much coffee the chipper young girl drank. She walked outside and found Pastor Richard pruning one of the lush green bushes.

"Good morning, Pastor. Ruth said I could find you out here."

"Well hello, Charlie. I haven't seen you since your grandmother's funeral. I'm glad you stopped by."

Charlie shifted her weight from one foot to another. Now that she was here, she didn't know what to say. "You have a way with plants, the garden is beautiful. It seems so peaceful here."

"Thank you! I have found taking care of this little patch of ground does wonders for my soul. Why don't we go sit by the fountain and talk? These old bones need a little break. "

Charlie followed the pastor to the fountain. A white iron cafe table set off to the side. "This is usually where I have my morning coffee. Let me text Ruth, and maybe she will bring us a cup out."

A few minutes later, the lively secretary brought out a tray with a carafe, two cups, and a variety of creamers along with some sugar.

Charlie stared at her cup. "Thank you for taking the time to see me."

"To tell the truth, my wife and I planned on paying you a visit after the holiday. I know things are difficult for you right now."

Charlie studied the man's face. He had been her grandmother's pastor for twenty-five years. He had started as a young man fresh out of seminary. Now, his hair was gray, and wrinkles lined eyes and mouth. A pair of glasses hung from the pocket of his red polo shirt. He looked more like a golfer with his khaki pants and brown loafers.

"You're welcome to visit anytime," Charlie said. "My grandmother thought very highly of you. I just wish she was here right now; she'd know what to do."

"She was a good woman," the pastor said. "But I can't help but wonder if she was here, would you let her in enough to help? The last time you were in trouble, you shut her out."

Charlie was surprised by his bluntness, but that's probably one of the reasons Betty Ann liked him. She appreciated straight talk and honest dialogue.

"She told you?" It was beginning to seem that Charlie's secret past wasn't much of a secret.

The pastor nodded. "Yes. At first, she was hurt, then worried. But long before your troubles, she had already accepted the fact that any relationship with you would be on your terms. She knew your pain ran deep and that the walls you put up were for your own self-preservation."

Charlie agreed. "She knew me well. Most people think it was my parents' accident that made me such a loner. But it wasn't. It just made me retreat deeper into myself."

"Is that when you stopped believing in God?" Pastor Richard asked.

Charlie thought for a moment. "I don't think I ever did believe in Him. He always seemed far away. Then, after the accident, I believed in Him only enough to be mad at Him. Everyone talks about how He's so loving and so good, but do you really want to know what I think? I think he doesn't like me very much. I take responsibility for my actions, my stupid mistakes. But my life has been one loss after another. The only explanation I can come up with is He either doesn't care or doesn't like me. Either way, it doesn't look good for me."

The pastor took a sip of his coffee. "I can see why you'd think that. But how do you feel now? Something in your thought process has changed, or you wouldn't be here."

"I guess I've been entertaining the thought that He could exist and that He does care. The funny thing is that it scares me more to believe in Him than it does to not believe."

"From what I know about you, that's not surprising," he said. "Belief requires a certain amount of hope and faith. You prefer things to be more tangible.

Charlie was impressed with his insight. "In my experience, hope and faith are dangerous."

Pastor Richard agreed. "You're not wrong. Believing in something greater than ourselves can be terrifying. If I might make a suggestion, explore the possibility that you've been wrong this whole time, and that God does care for you. In fact, dare to ponder the thought that He gave His Son to die so that you might live. Go back and re-read your Bible, but this time replace your skepticism with possibility. Tell me, what would be the worst that could happen?"

Charlie smiled. "You reminded me of my dad just then. He knew my doubts and always encouraged me to look at both sides of things. In all things, not just matters regarding faith. He was a smart man, and I admired him greatly. Pastor, I know the Bible. I've never pretended to be a good person. I know that forgiveness is a big part of this, and I'm not sure I qualify for any type of forgiveness."

"Who does? That's where grace comes in. And the beauty of grace is that we don't get what we deserve, but what we need. I've talked to many different people in many different places in their life's journey. And the thing I've learned is that no one is out of the reach of grace. God is always just one step away. He doesn't walk too far behind or too far ahead. Think about what I've said."

"I promise I will," Charlie said.

"Good. Now that that's settled, Virginia will have me in the dog house if

I don't invite you to our house for lunch after church on Sunday. Every year she puts on a spread. We're having some other folks over to watch the parade of boats, then the fireworks later on."

Charlie surprised herself by agreeing to attend. "I would love to. I'll see you on Sunday."

"We look forward to seeing you and if you need us for anything, please, don't hesitate to call."

"Thank you, Pastor." Charlie walked back across the lawn with a feeling of cautious optimism. As she walked up the back steps of her apartment, she heard yelling. When she walked in, she heard Wren's voice from down the hall. She had given the lawyer a key so she could come and go from her office as needed. Charlie stood at the door as Wren yelled into her cell phone.

"He told Detective Holiday she didn't do it. You can't possibly.... Counselor, check your toes. They're very close to the line of malicious prosecution. Good day!"

Wren paced the floor a minute before acknowledging Charlie. "Don't you miss the days of being able to slam the phone down when you hang up on someone? A whole generation will never experience that satisfaction, and I find that very sad."

Charlie laughed. "For a minute, I thought I was going to have to come up with bail money for you."

Wren shook her head. "Hoke Dodd is a pain. He's refusing to drop the attempted murder charges. He's insinuating that Andy's covering for you and that they are standing by the eyewitness statement. The truth is, because the gun is linked to both crimes, if he drops the attempted murder charge, then it's going to be hard to prove you murdered Kevin since Andy's shooter had the gun."

"Wren! That's great news!"

Wren raised an eyebrow "Are you sure you heard me correctly?"

"Yes!" Charlie was excited. "If we can get the gun thrown out, then their case falls apart."

Wren didn't share Charlie's enthusiasm. "Charlie, they found the gun in your apartment with your fingerprints on it and gun residue on your hands and clothes."

Charlie shrugged. "I didn't say it was going to be easy to do. But it's not impossible."

"I see your wheels turning," Wren said. "What are you thinking?"

Charlie began to pace. "We've concentrated on Kevin, but I still think we need to check out the girlfriend. It would make sense that she'd be in on it since they came to Holiday Cove together. She'd have a motive to kill Kevin if she thought he was double-crossing her and if she was in Andy's office, she must think there's mention of her in his files."

Wren nodded. "Then we'll find her and get to the bottom of this. We need Andy's files."

"It looks like I'll need to delay my first day back at work. I'm headed over to the hospital," Charlie said.

"Don't go empty-handed."

Charlie smiled as she thought of chocolate donuts with sprinkles. Lots of sprinkles. Something that felt like hope sprouted in her heart.

Twenty-Three

What are you doing?" Charlie stood in the doorway of Andy's hospital room with a box of donuts and two cups of coffee as he struggled to put his shirt on.

"I'm bustin' out of this joint. You gonna just stand there or help me?" He said in his best James Cagney voice.

Charlie strode across the room and put breakfast on the tray. "You've watched too many old movies. Did your doctor say you could leave?"

"He didn't say I couldn't. Of course, I haven't seen him yet this morning," Andy grinned.

"Andy! You can't just walk out of the hospital two days after you've been shot!"

"Why not? I feel fine. My blood levels are normal. I'm just a little sore. That's all."

"They aren't going to let you leave," Charlie said.

"They can't make me stay," Andy replied.

Charlie threw up her hands in exasperation. "Just why are you in such a hurry to get out?"

"You mean besides the bad food and lumpy bed?" Andy asked.

Charlie pointed to the box of donuts she had laid down. "I brought you donuts, so the food is no excuse."

Andy grabbed one. "You got me extra sprinkles. I knew you cared."

"You have the taste buds of a five-year-old," Charlie chastised.

"It keeps me young. Would you hand me my shoes, please?"

Charlie threw a pair of loafers at him. Andy ducked.

"Missed me. Now, are you helping me out of here or not?"

Charlie crossed her arms. "Only if you tell me the real reason you're so desperate to get out."

"Fine," Andy said. "I want to go see Lance and find out where he is on my case."

Charlie huffed. "I'll tell you where he's at. Right where he's always been with his finger pointing at me. The DA didn't drop the charges against me."

"They don't believe me," Andy said. "That's not a good sign for either of us."

"I know," Charlie agreed. "Maybe it's time you start looking for a lawyer."

Andy walked towards the door. "Not yet. We're going to see Lance together and talk some sense into him!"

Charlie waited while Andy signed discharge papers and got a speech about leaving against doctor's orders. After everything was settled at the hospital, they drove to the police station. Lance didn't look happy to see them walk into his office.

"Before you say anything, it's out of my hands," he said. "The DA's callin' the shots."

Andy and Charlie sat down across the cold gray desk from Lance. He looked like he hadn't slept in a week. His clothes were rumpled, and dark bags drooped under his eyes. Charlie noticed a cot in the corner of the small office.

"The district attorney took their cue from you," Charlie reminded him. "You've never really looked for another suspect except me, and now you've placed Andy under the microscope."

Lance pointed a finger at Andy. "You're the one that thought your boyfriend here was capable of murder, don't be layin' that one at my feet."

Charlie shouted. "At least I can admit when I'm wrong! You'd rather chew nails than admit you've been wrong about both of us! It looks like that's working out well for you too. That cot over there looks really comfy!"

Lance's face turned a dozen shades of red. "That's none of your business! If all you did was come here to yell at me, you can walk right back out the way you come in!"

Andy whistled loudly. "Time out!" The office got quiet. "Everybody just needs to take a deep breath." Andy looked at Lance. "I just have one question. Do you think Charlie did any of this? She's your friend, man and she's like a sister to your wife. Is there any part of you that really thinks she's guilty?"

Lance blew out a gust of air and clasped his beefy hands behind his head.

"It's not that simple."

"Yes, it is," Andy said. "If you don't do something, they are going to send her to prison, and she's innocent. We can't let that happen!"

Lance looked helpless. "There's nothing I can do."

"Yes, there is," Andy replied. "You've got resources and connections. This goes all the way back to Jack Marsden. Get us some information on his visitors while he was in prison. Find out some more about the escape attempt. I think he was coming after Charlie and since he didn't make it, whoever was helping him came here to finish what Jack started."

Charlie took the picture of Kevin's girlfriend out of her purse. "This is Kevin Wilson's girlfriend. I think she was in on it and I think she shot Andy because there's something about her in those files. Andy didn't give Kevin the information on me, this girl did. I've been racking my brain trying to figure out why she looks so familiar. Send a copy of this picture to the prison. See if anyone recognizes her. Please, Lance."

Lance took the piece of paper. "I see you've been talkin' to Jonas. I'll help you two, but I'll be honest, I don't think it's goin' to do much good. Andy, you'll be lucky if you don't end up sittin' at the defendant's table beside her. Dodd read my files on the case. He agrees with my theory that you were behind the blackmail. If they can find proof, they're gonna charge you. In fact, after Charlie, you're their number one suspect for Kevin's murder."

Andy shook his head. "Nice to know you always see the best in people."

"I'm not gonna apologize for doin' my job, Andy. I went where the evidence pointed me," Lance said.

Andy tried not to shout. "Yeah, but did you ever once stop to think you were going in the wrong direction? People's lives are at stake. I can't worry about myself right. We have to prove Charlie's innocence. We're going to the bank. The information the killer was looking for is in my safety deposit box. Then, we're going to take it to Charlie's and go over it with a fine-tooth comb."

Lance rubbed his temples. "Charlie, I do believe you're in danger, and they're not going to let me offer you any protection. But I'll make sure our increased patrols for the holiday include a swing by your place at least once an hour. Make sure your alarms are set and maybe even ask Susan or Wren to stay with you for a few days. I'm sure Nan would volunteer, too."

Charlie knew how hard it was for the straight-laced Lance to tiptoe into the grey areas of life. "Thank you. But I think you and Nan might need some time together without mention of my name. If I remember correctly, your last date was interrupted. I'll check with Wren and Susan."

"What about me?" Andy asked.

Charlie shook her head. "Tongues are wagging enough about my life as it is. I will not have Holiday Cove's most eligible bachelor sleeping under my roof, adding fuel to the fire."

Andy tried not to look hurt. Charlie was used to fighting her own battles, and he wasn't going to push the issue.

"Fair enough. Lance is my office still a crime scene, or can I stop by and get a few things?"

"They finished up last night. But you may want to have it cleaned."

"I'll have time. I'll be staying at my office until I know Charlie's safe."

Charlie looked at Andy. "That's not going to be very comfortable."

"Are you kidding? I have everything I need, a bathroom with a shower, a microwave, a fridge, and I'm sure Lance here will let me borrow his cot."

The red returned to Lance's face. "Very funny. Wait until you two are married. Then come at me with your jokes."

Charlie and Andy looked at Lance dumbstruck. He just whistled as he walked out of the room.

Twenty-Four

neither Andy nor Charlie mentioned Lance's marriage comment as they drove to Andy's office. The town was already buzzing with people, and Charlie had trouble finding a parking space. The smell of bleach and Pine-Sol hit them as soon as they opened the door to the office, and they heard voices coming from the back room. Andy motioned for Charlie to get behind him as they padded down the hallway. The door to his office was open, so he peered in.

"Mrs. Hayes! What are you doing back?" Andy asked.

"Andy Brock! I have a bone to pick with you!" The spry senior threw a sponge in a bucket of water and used a nearby chair to help her lift herself off the floor. "Why is it that I had to hear about you almost being killed from Lou Guthrie?"

Charlie poked her head in the office while Mrs. Hayes read Andy the riot act. She had taken her gloves off and had one hand on her hip while the other hand pointed a pudgy little finger at Andy. Her usual office attire had been replaced with a brightly colored floral smock and a pair of black polyester stretch pants. A pink kerchief covered her short, grey permed curls. Her face turned an even brighter shade of red when she saw Charlie.

"And what are you doing here? Haven't you caused enough trouble? You're going to get him killed!"

"Mrs. Hayes, please calm down. Have a seat, and I'll get you a lemonade. Who is this that you have with you?" Andy asked.

Mrs. Hayes huffed and puffed, but she took a seat in one of the chairs and motioned the other woman in the room to join her.

"This is my sister, Reva. She insisted on coming back here with me when I found out you were hurt."

Reva waved. "Nice to meet y'all." She looked almost identical to Mrs. Hayes except for her platinum blonde curls. "Marcy brags on her Andy all the time."

Andy blushed as he left to go get the ladies a drink from the break room.

Reva turned to Charlie. "And who might you be?"

Before Charlie could answer, Mrs. Hayes jumped in. "This is the one I was telling you about. Trouble with a capital T."

Charlie shook Reva's hand. "I'm Charlie. Nice to meet you."

Reva winked. "Don't mind Marcy. Nobody's good enough for Andy in her eyes."

"Oh, we're not together like that," Charlie explained.

Reva winked at Charlie again and then whispered. "That's what I'd say too in front of Marcy. You're smart and pretty. No wonder she doesn't like you."

Charlie opened her mouth to object but decided it wouldn't be worth the hassle. Andy made it back with the drinks and surveyed the room.

"What are you two lovely ladies up to?" He asked.

Mrs. Hayes began to flail her arms about again. "Those police officers left this place a mess! There's blood everywhere, and papers all strewn about. There's fingerprint dust on all my nice furniture. We run a respectable place of business here. I won't have people coming in here seeing it like this."

"Mrs. Hayes, no one's coming," Andy explained. "I'm shutting the office down for a few days, just until things calm down. Why don't you and Reva go enjoy this beautiful day? I'll finish cleaning later."

"We will not!" Mrs. Hayes leapt from her chair. "You and Ms. Trouble just do whatever you need to do and leave us to our work."

Andy looked at Charlie and shrugged. "Just give me ten minutes to shower and change into something that doesn't smell like a ten-year-old tennis shoe."

"I'll wait for you out front," Charlie said. "Nice to meet you, Reva. Have a nice day, Mrs. Hayes." Charlie dashed from the room without waiting for a reply. A few minutes later, Andy emerged. He didn't look like a man who had just been playing a round of cards with death. He had trimmed his beard, and his silver hair was still damp from the shower. He could have been on a yacht commercial in his navy blue polo, khaki pants, and boat shoes.

"Let's get out of here before I hear another lecture," he grabbed Charlie's arm as they rushed out the door.

They made it to the bank and back to Charlie's before lunch. The parking lot of the Vintage Gypsy was empty. Charlie and Andy stopped downstairs before going up to the apartment. Mr. Bear barked as they entered the store. Susan and the rest of the staff were busy cleaning up and restocking where they could.

"Wow! You guys must have had a busy morning!" Charlie said.

Susan wiped a tiny bit of sweat from her forehead. "We have and will probably have an even busier afternoon." She looked at Andy. "Glad to see you back in the land of the living."

"You have no idea how good it is to be back," he smiled.

"Susan," Charlie said. "Why don't you take the gang over to Lunch on the Lawn and enjoy some time away from this place. I can hold the fort down here for a while."

"Are you sure? She asked. "I don't like the thought of leaving you alone."

Charlie nodded. "I'm not alone. Andy's here, and it looks like everyone else is at the courthouse. See if Wren wants to go, too. She's been working too hard."

"Good idea. We'll bring you something back," Susan promised.

After everyone left, Andy settled in the kitchen with the paperwork he'd retrieved from the bank and Charlie did a walkthrough of the store. She'd need to make another trip to the storage shed soon. As she was walking back to the front, she almost bumped into Lance.

"I'm sorry. I didn't hear you come in."

"Where's everyone at?" Lance asked.

"I gave them a break," Charlie answered. "We weren't busy. Andy's in the kitchen going over his notes."

"Can you close the store for a few minutes? I've got some information."

Charlie hoped it was good news for a change. "Sure. Go on back to the kitchen. I'll be there in a minute."

She locked the front door and placed the closed sign in the window then joined Andy and Lance in the kitchen. They were digging through Andy's paperwork like madmen. Charlie sat down.

"What's going on?" She asked.

"One of the guards recognized your picture of the girl," Lance said. "She visited Jack frequently; the last time was the day before his escape attempt. The name she signed in with was Olivia Hollister. We're looking to see if Andy has any record of anyone by that name."

"Here it is!" Andy held up a piece of paper and started to read. The excitement in his voice turning to disappointment. "Another dead end. Looks like Jack had been married before when he was younger. After the divorce, she went back to her maiden name, Hollister. She died while Jack was on trial. Cancer."

"But why would someone be using his dead wife's name to visit him?" Charlie asked in frustration. "That makes no sense." She picked up the picture she had drawn of the mystery woman. "I know I've seen this face." Something finally clicked. She rummaged through the photos scattered across the table. She found the one she was looking for and grabbed Andy's laptop. After a few seconds, she turned the computer around to face Andy and Lance. "This is Olivia Hollister." Charlie had found her obituary online.

They both stared. "She looks like your drawing," Andy said.

"That's because Olivia had a daughter," Charlie pointed at the picture she had found. "This girl."

Lance picked up the picture and studied it. "This is your trial."

Charlie nodded. "Take a close look at the girl behind the defendant's table. She was there every day of my trial. I could feel her staring at the back of my head. I just didn't connect the dots. That's Mallory Hollister, Olivia's daughter, and Kevin's girlfriend. Looks like we found our mystery woman."

Twenty-Five

Wren and Susan walked into the kitchen. "Why is the door locked and the Closed sign in the window?" Susan asked. "We have a string of traffic coming."

"Oh my gosh! I forgot! Y'all won't believe it! Guys, fill them in while I open the store back up." Charlie ran from the kitchen.

The Open sign was barely turned on before the crowds rushed in. Susan came out of the kitchen to help. The last customer finally walked out of the door an hour after normal closing. Susan, Charlie, and Mr. Bear climbed the stairs to the apartment to join the others that had moved operations upstairs. Wren's office had exploded onto Charlie's kitchen table. Paperwork was everywhere. Andy was jumping back and forth between his laptop and a stack of papers, Lance was in corner barking orders into a phone, and Wren was madly scribbling on a legal note pad.

"My kitchen looks like a war room!" Charlie didn't know whether to laugh or cry. "Y'all are aware it's past six, right?"

Lance came back into the kitchen. "My lovely wife is. She is not one bit happy about being left out of the loop. She's on her way over with supper. She stopped by Mae Lin's for some Chinese food and will be here in about thirty minutes expecting to be brought up to speed. Charlie, you got a fax in this place? We got some more information on Mallory coming."

"Sure. The number is 555-9612."

Lance left the kitchen again barking more orders into the phone.

Charlie looked around the room and was filled with sudden emotion. These people were her friends, and they were doing everything in their power to save her. She felt humbled and ashamed that she had spent her life keeping people out. She composed herself before she started crying in front of everybody.

"Susan, you have to be exhausted," Charlie said. "Why don't you go home and get some rest?"

Susan shook her head. "No way. We finally have something good happening, and I'm not going anywhere."

Charlie understood her excitement. "Then at least call Brett and have him come over for supper."

"That I can do," Susan agreed.

"Okay, guys, we need to clear the table, so we have somewhere to eat," Charlie said. While the others cleared the table, she changed clothes and got Mr. Bear settled in for the evening.

By the time Nan and Brett arrived, everyone had washed up and set the table. Nan brought enough food to feed an army. The table was loaded with noodles, egg rolls, pot stickers, rice, and three main entrees.

"I know you were busy today, Charlie, but all this news and no phone call?" Nan pouted. "But at least Lance is finally on the right side of things."

Charlie hugged her friend and whispered. "Andy took his cot, so you have to let him come home tonight."

Nan punched her friend in the arm. "Let's eat."

Lance came to the table with the fax he'd been waiting for.

"What does it say?" Charlie asked.

"Did Jack ever mention having a daughter?" He asked.

Charlie shook her head. "He never talked about his family at all."

"It took some diggin', but we found the birth certificate. Looks like Mallory is Jack's daughter too. Olivia had full custody and doesn't look like Jack was in the picture very much. He paid his child support on time but had no contact with her until she showed up usin' her mama's name at the prison."

"What other information do we have on her?" Charlie asked.

"Not much," Lance answered. "The last time she used the name Mallory Hollister was when she graduated college, two years after Jack was sent to prison. She majored in Forensic Science."

"That would come in handy if you ever wanted to frame someone for murder," Nan quipped.

Lance continued. "After graduation, she just disappears. My guess is she changed her name. With the kind of money these people have, it would have been easy to become a whole new person."

"She could be anybody," Charlie got a chill. "And she's after me."

Lance nodded. "They'd been plotting Jack's escape and revenge for over ten years. When he got killed, I think she continued his plan. When you decided to stay in Holiday Cove, you became an easy target. With the internet, she could keep up with all that happened here. She knew when your grandmother died, and she knew you thought it was safe to stay here. I think that's when she set her plan in motion."

"But why hasn't anyone seen her?" Susan asked.

Andy spoke up. "I think the fight at the motel was staged to give Kevin a viable reason to be in Holiday Cove. Afterward, she changed her appearance, possibly even with plastic surgery since she could afford it. Then came to Holiday Cove at a later time, looking completely different with no ties to Kevin. She secretly fed Kevin the information to blackmail Charlie. But either something went wrong, and she killed him, or she'd always planned to get rid of him after he'd served his purpose."

"I don't think it matters," Lance said. "Mallory saw an opportunity to frame Charlie, and she took it. Charlie was at Kevin's the night he was murdered. She dropped her gun, and either Mallory or Kevin found it, then later, Mallory shot him with it."

A sad smile crept across Charlie's face. "I'm sorry I lied to you all. I was afraid it would be like last time with no one believing me. If I admitted I was at Kevin's that night, it would look bad. I was trying to figure things out on my own and just made it all worse. I went back the next day to look for the gun after Lance made me realize I'd lost it. That's when I found Kevin's box of blackmail letters."

"Then how did Lance end up with them?" Andy asked.

Again, Charlie was embarrassed. "Someone broke in while I was out at dinner. I couldn't say anything to anyone because I wasn't supposed to have them."

"So Mallory's been able to break into your twice house?" Nan asked.

"Three times if you count the garage," Charlie said. "She had to be the one that planted the gun and the hoodie here the night of Andy's shooting."

"I still don't understand why she wanted to kill Andy," Susan said.

Andy replied. "I don't think she wanted to kill me. She just wanted to see what information I had. When I came into the office, I surprised her."

"Right now, we need to concentrate on how she's getting into Charlie's house," Nan persisted.

"I think I know," Brett said. He had been listening intently to the conversation. "My crew installed the alarm system. It's an upgrade I offer. If Kevin knew what he was doing, he could have figured out Charlie's code and given it to Mallory."

"Then we need to change that code, now," Lance said.

Brett stood up to make a call. "I'll take care of it."

"If Mallory figures out we've found out her secret, Charlie's life is in danger," Nan said. "We need to make sure she's not alone. I've got an overnight bag in the car and plan on taking the first shift."

Charlie smiled. "Tomorrow is a busy day, but we're closing at noon to get ready for the Stars and Stripes Gala."

"I'll be your escort for the evening," Andy said.

Charlie arched an eyebrow. "Are you sure you're well enough?"

Andy grinned. "I dare anybody to say differently."

"I've added this block to the patrol route tonight," Lance said. "Tomorrow, we'll continue to work on finding out Mallory's new identity."

Brett came back with the new code for the alarm system. After making sure it worked, everyone began to say their goodbyes. Andy lingered to help Charlie finish cleaning up.

"Don't forget to set the alarm with the new code Brett gave you," he said.

"I won't."

" And don't forget to lock the doors when Nan comes back in."

"I won't," Charlie replied. "Anything else you want to nag me about before you leave?"

Andy's eyes twinkled. "What color dress are you wearing tomorrow night?"

Charlie laughed. "I don't know. Why do you care?"

"So I can match you, of course! It'll be like the prom we never had. I'll even get you a corsage and everything."

He inched closer. Charlie tilted her face up. "I'll let you know as soon as I decide."

Andy leaned down.

"Charlie! Andy! Come quick!"

Nan was breathless. Fire engines sounded in the background. Charlie and Andy ran outside. A massive fire roared in the distance. Lance walked up to the small group.

"Charlie, I'm sorry. Cove storage just went up in flames.

"No!" Charlie screamed. "No!"

She watched the flames flicker against the dark sky as her world went up in smoke.

Twenty-Six

L ance wouldn't let them drive out to the storage facility because it was still too dangerous. Charlie told Susan to call the other employees and tell them not to come in the next morning. It would mean losing a lot of money, but she needed time to figure out her next step. If the store had another big day of sales, she'd be entirely out of stock. Andy finally left after she had calmed down. She was thankful for insurance, but it would only cover the money, not the time it would take to regain all she had lost. Her collection spanned years.

After trying and failing to sleep, she decided to get up and start a pot of coffee. The fire should be all the way out by now, and she wanted to go see the damage. Mr. Bear followed her into the kitchen, eagerly awaiting his breakfast. Charlie tried to be quiet so she wouldn't wake Nan. They had gone to bed late, and Nan would be expected at the Holiday mansion to help get everything in place for the night's event. Charlie tried to be excited about the Gala, but she was just too tired. Her mind kept returning to the moment Nan had come rushing in the room last night. Had Andy been about to kiss her?

Her feelings for Andy needed to be sorted out, but she didn't even know where to start. In the span of a week, they'd gone from friends to enemies, thinking the worst about the other, and then a missed kiss. It was a roller coaster ride, and she needed to get off. She didn't even know if she could be in a relationship. After Jack, there had been no one, a few flings here and there, but no connections. She thought of Pastor Richard's words on the walls she had built up. Almost every decision Charlie had made in her life was to benefit herself, to protect herself. Keeping people at arm's length made sure she didn't get hurt, but was she really living?

She also remembered she had made a promise to read the Bible. She tiptoed into the sunroom and found her grandmother's Bible on the bookshelf. She picked it up, and something fell out. Charlie retrieved it from the floor. It was an envelope with her name on it in her grandmother's handwriting. Her hands shook as she broke the seal.

My Dearest Charlie,

You are holding in your hands the greatest Book ever written. It has brought me comfort and peace even in times of sorrow. I hope it will do the same for you now. I am writing this on the night I was told I didn't have much longer to live. My first thoughts were of your grandfather and your parents. Soon, I will see them once more. And I will finally get to see my Jesus face to face. I have waited for that moment my whole life. I know that me going home leaves you here alone. I pray that you find your hope here in these pages as I did. I know you feel like your past disqualifies you from the love of Jesus. But nothing could be further from the truth. Nothing can separate you from His love. And when you read His word, you'll see that I'm right. He offered His life for all, no exceptions.

On this earth, you have been one of the greatest joys of my life. I have watched you grow into a strong, independent woman. But I know some of your choices haunt you, that you have let shame and guilt dictate your life now. I want you to know, I love you no less. You are a part of me. We all fail. We all fall. Don't believe the lie that you are unforgivable, unlovable. Don't let your past continue to eat at your spirit until there's nothing left. You know what to do. You've always known. If you're reading this, it means you're finally in the right place. I love you, my child.

Teardrops fell on the paper, and Charlie's heart felt like it was going to explode. What would happen if she let go? She clenched her hand into a fist and then opened it. She felt the tug on her heart. Her grandmother was right, she'd always known what to do. She had finally come to the end of herself. She slid to the floor on her knees and buried her head into the couch cushion. For several minutes, she could only muster a few words. "God, please forgive me. Forgive me." Soon it all came out. A flood of wrongs laid at the foot of the cross. "It should have been me, but you took my place. You died for me. You came back for me. I don't deserve it." The realization of the need for a Savior overwhelmed her. She was not alone. He was waiting. "Save me," she whispered. "I surrender whatever is left of this life to you." Charlie didn't know how long she stayed there on the floor. She didn't want the moment to end. For the first time in her life, she felt free.

"Charlie, what are you doing?" Nan walked in and sat on the floor beside her.

Charlie lifted her head. "Talking to God."

Nan smiled. "Let's talk to him together."

The two girls prayed together for a few more minutes until Mr. Bear began barking.

"Somebody's ready for a walk," Charlie stood.

"I'll start breakfast," Nan said. "Lance will be over in a few minutes with more news about Mallory."

Charlie took Mr. Bear outside and saw Pastor Richard in the garden. Charlie broke out into a run.

"Pastor! Good morning!" Charlie was out of breath by the time she and Mr. Bear got to the garden.

"Charlie! Good Morning!" Pastor Richard smiled. " You look like you're just bursting at the seams to tell me something."

"I did what you said. I opened up the Bible last night. My grandmother had left a letter there for me. She never stopped believing in me or loving me. I knew I needed Jesus in my life. I believe. I'm not alone anymore."

Pastor Richard clapped his hands together. "That's an answered prayer! Tomorrow will truly be a celebration."

"I'm looking forward to it. Thank you for all your prayers," Charlie said. "And if you don't mind, keep them coming. We still have a lot of work to do to get me out of all this trouble."

"I promise I won't stop."

The pastor waved as Charlie and Mr. Bear walked back across the lawn. As they neared the back steps, Lance pulled into the driveway.

"Hey, Lance. Come on up, Nan's cooking breakfast although I have no idea what we're having. My cupboards are bare."

"Well, as long as it's edible, I'm famished," he said.

"Look who I found!" Charlie said as they entered the apartment.

"Just in time!" Nan yelled from the kitchen.

"Yum! I can't remember the last time I had french toast," Charlie said.

They all sat down to eat. Nan prayed, and they dug in.

"What's the news?" Nan asked.

"I got to thinkin' last night. We could try to track down females that moved into the area within the last twelve to twenty-four months. We're short staffed right now because of the holidays, but I'll put someone on it first thing Monday mornin'."

"That's a great idea!" Charlie said. "Is it clear enough for me to go down to the storage building this morning?"

"It is, but I have to warn you, there's not much left," Lance said. "The fire chief is pretty sure it's arson."

"Do you think it could have been Mallory?" Nan asked.

Lance shrugged his shoulders. "I don't want to blame every crime in Holiday Cove on her, but with Charlie's stuff bein' there, she's high on my list of suspects. I don't want you goin' anywhere alone. Who's goin' to be your shadow today after Nan leaves?"

"Andy's going to the storage building with me," Charlie said. "Then Wren will be here the rest of the day."

"Just be careful," Lance warned.

"I promise."

They finished breakfast, and Charlie got ready to go see what was left of her business.

Twenty-Seven

Andy and Charlie explored what was left in the storage building. What the fire hadn't damaged, the water had. They managed to salvage a few pieces of jewelry, some old knives, and a few other odds and ends. Charlie cried at the destruction. Rare books, period clothing, valuable ceramics and pottery, all broken and burned to ash. Irreplaceable pieces of treasure now nothing but smoke.

Andy put his arm around her. "I'll help you any way I can. You can teach me how to be a picker. I'll even go out on your first trip with you."

Charlie cried into his shoulder. In the middle of nothing, he still had hope. She was grateful for his strength.

"I think that's an excellent plan," Charlie said. "Now, take me home so I can figure out what I'm wearing tonight."

Wren was already there by the time they arrived back at the apartment.

"Hey! Were you able to save anything?" She asked.

Charlie dumped a small pile on the table. "Not exactly."

"Well, I've been on the computer all morning. I know a large part of picking is the thrill of the hunt, but you don't have that time right now. So, I've tracked down a couple of things that might interest you." Wren sat the laptop down in front of Charlie. "A client of mine just inherited this property. It's acres and acres of a picker's dream. There are at least three big barns, and a dozen sheds filled to the brim with stuff! He said to take what you want, and as quickly as you can so, he can start developing it."

"Wren! This could at least get us back up and running while I went on some road trips."

Andy cleared his throat. "We. While we go on some road trips."

Charlie laughed. "While we go on some road trips. Wren, if you ever get out of the law business, there's a place for you here."

"I can't retire until we make sure you don't go to jail," Wren said.

"I have faith in you," Charlie said. "But tonight everyone is taking a break and enjoying the gala. Charlie handed Wren an invitation. "We'll go downstairs and pick out our dresses. It'll be fun."

Andy stood to leave. "Don't forget to text me colors, Prom Queen."

Charlie blushed. "I won't. I'll see you this evening."

"Five sharp," Andy reminded her. "I'll be here to pick you up."

After he left, Wren, Charlie, and Mr. Bear went downstairs. Thankfully there was still a couple of racks of gowns for Wren and Charlie to choose from. From the depletion in stock, Charlie felt a lot of people would be wearing vintage couture from the Vintage Gypsy. Wren found her outfit first, a white chiffon sleeveless blouse with a draped cowl neckline, a navy satin skirt, and a simple red satin sash to tie everything together.

"It's perfect for you!" Charlie said.

"I think so, too. Now let's find yours."

They looked for a few minutes.

"Eureka! Charlie, only you can pull this one off!" Wren held up a gown for Charlie to inspect. It wasn't her typical style. The bold sixties gown had three gathered panels of red, white, and blue. It was strapless with an empire waist, and Charlie loved the organza material.

"You're right!" Charlie squealed in excitement. "This is it! I'm texting Andy a picture."

The girls spent the rest of the afternoon getting ready. Charlie went all out with her sixties look, applying striking eye make-up and nude lipstick. She piled her hair on top of her head in a bold bun and crowned it with a small tiara encrusted with red, clear, and blue glass.

Charlie was impressed with Wren's look although it was odd seeing the lawyer wearing makeup. She looked sophisticated with her strawberry hair tied in an elegant chignon. The skirt flattered her petite frame and made her look like a tiny doll. Her long mascara-coated eyelashes and pink lip gloss accentuated her delicate features.

Wren refused to ride to the gala with Charlie and Andy.

"I'm not being a third wheel," she said. She grabbed her satin evening bag and walked toward the door.

"It's not a date," Charlie tried to convince her, but Wren just laughed.

"Poor Cupid has his work cut out with you two knuckleheads. See you at the party!" And with that, she breezed out the door. Charlie could hear her laughing to herself all the way down the stairs.

She had just finished putting Mr. Bear in his kennel when the doorbell rang. Andy stood at the door with a beautiful corsage of red and white tea roses.

"Come in," Charlie said. "I'm almost ready."

"Almost? You look stunning. What else could you possibly need to do?"

She felt like a silly school girl when he looked at her that way. And he didn't look too bad himself. Not many men could pull off a white suit. But it was perfectly tailored, and the navy shirt brought out the blue in his eyes. The stars and stripes bow tie was a cute touch.

"You and Mr. Bear have the same bowtie," Charlie grinned.

"Well, then I must be up on the latest fashion since Mr. Bear is the best-dressed dog in the county."

"Is that for me?" Charlie pointed at the corsage.

"It is," Andy answered. "But I have no idea where to pin it."

Charlie shook her head and took it from him. "Have a seat, I'll put this on and finish getting ready. Give me five minutes."

Andy waited patiently until Charlie emerged fifteen minutes later with the corsage pinned at the top of her dress. Andy beamed at the sight of her.

"I don't think you understand how long five minutes is," he quipped.

"Yes, I do," she fired back. "It's as long as I need it to be."

He knew better than to argue. "Come on, Cinderella, your carriage awaits."

They walked outside, and Charlie expected to see Andy's old truck. Instead, in its place was a sixty-two white Alpha Romeo Spider with red-rimmed tires. Charlie clapped her hands.

"Andy, it's perfect! How in the world did you get this?"

Andy opened the door for her. "I rented this baby for the whole weekend."

Charlie eased herself into the passenger seat. She truly did feel like Cinderella going to the ball. She just hoped she didn't turn into a pumpkin at midnight.

Twenty-Eight

The Holiday mansion was a sight to see. The great white Victorian was almost three times the size of Charlie's. It sat upon a perfectly manicured luxurious green lawn with Lake Holiday as its back yard. Three grand porches were covered in red, white, and blue bunting. Andy pulled up to the front drive and helped Charlie out of the car. He handed the valet the keys and walked with Charlie into the foyer. People were milling around the ballroom before making their way to the terrace where a band played slow jazz. Buffet tables were loaded with shrimp cocktails, barbeque, desserts, and every other type of food that could be desired. Round tables covered with pristine white table cloths surrounded a make-shift dance floor. Charlie saw Susan waving to get her attention. She and Andy made their way through the crowd to the table not far from the dance floor. Charlie was surprised to see Susan in a color other than black. She had even worn her hair down. It fell in sleek ebony waves over her pale shoulders. The bright red mermaid dress accentuated her thin frame. She had even managed to get Brett into formal attire although the bear of a man looked uncomfortable in his navy blue suit and red button up. Wren sat beside them and smiled as Charlie and Andy approached.

"I knew you'd be late," she giggled

"Charlie goes by her own clock," Andy shrugged.

"Have you seen Nan?" Susan asked. "She is the queen of the ball. I bet her dress cost more than I make in a year."

"I haven't seen her or Lance," Charlie replied. "He was going to try and see if he could do some more digging on Mallory."

"I propose we enjoy the evening," Andy said. "Let's give Charlie a night off from murder and mayhem."

The group agreed. Charlie squeezed Andy's hand underneath the table. For tonight, she would enjoy the moment.

Nan finally made her way to the table. Susan was right. That dress must have cost a small fortune. Nan looked like a Greek goddess. Her hair cascaded in golden curls down one side of her face. A sea of carnelian chiffon draped over one shoulder and flowed down to her ankles. The strapless gown dripped with ruby rhinestones. As she got closer to the table, Charlie could see her face was as red as her gown. She sat down sullenly as she motioned for one of the servers to bring her a tea.

"Lance just called. Apparently, he's found something big that he can't pull himself away from. I can't believe he's missing the gala! And of course, his mother blames me like it's somehow my fault."

"Oh, Nan, I'm sorry," Charlie said. "I feel guilty for asking, but do you know if it had to do with my case?"

"Yes, he's not working on anything else. He thinks he's got a lead on Mallory's identity here."

"Really?" Charlie was excited. "That would change everything."

"So much for taking the night off from murder and mayhem," Andy joked.

Nan smiled. "I really shouldn't complain. He's working hard to prove Charlie is innocent."

"And for that, I am eternally grateful," Charlie said.

Nan took a sip of her iced tea. "I'll try to make it back over here later. But I better be off greeting our other guests before Mother Holiday begins another rampage. And don't y'all sit here all night either! Get out there on the dance floor and have some fun! That's an order!"

Andy turned to Charlie. "Let's not make the boss mad. May I have this dance?"

Charlie held out her hand. "You may."

A slow jazz song played in the background as the couple began to sway to the beat. Andy held her close, and Charlie laid her head on his shoulder. She could feel his breath on her hair. For the first time since she could remember, she thought she was where she belonged. In this man's arms. In this town. Hope fluttered in her chest. She wondered if Andy could feel her pounding heart. No words passed between them because none were needed. A lifetime of unspoken feelings had their own language. Maybe it was that moment of peace, or maybe because for the first time since recent events unfolded her mind wasn't racing, the image of the girl in Charlie's drawing popped into her head again. She had seen that face here. Tonight. It was on the edge of Charlie's memory. She just needed a minute alone. She hated to stop the moment with Andy, but she needed to.

"Andy, I need something to cool off. I'm going to see if I can track me down one of those iced teas."

Andy pulled back. "You're not trying to run off, are you?" He looked hurt.

Charlie grabbed both of his hands. "No, my days of running are over. I'm right where I belong. I know my timing stinks. I'm just crazy thirsty all of a sudden. Go join the others back at the table and I'll be right back. Five minutes."

Andy shook his head. "Five minutes, my foot. Why don't you go sit down, and I'll bring us both something to drink?"

Charlie held up five fingers. "Five minutes. I promise I'll be right back."

Andy relented. While he rejoined their friends, Charlie walked into the cool of the air-conditioned mansion. She began scanning the faces in the ballroom, hoping something would jog her memory.

"Lord, help me remember," Charlie breathed a silent prayer. She walked away from the crowded room into a small sitting parlor down the hall. She sat in the dark and closed her eyes. She let her mind drift over the last week, looking for that face. Her eyes flicked open. It couldn't be. Charlie racked her brain. Mallory was there all the time. She had to get to Andy.

She got up to leave, but a shadowed figure walked into the room. The door closed, and Charlie heard the sound of the lock clicking into place.

Twenty-Nine

Do you really think after all you've taken from me that I would let you take him away from me, too?" The figure said.

Charlie reached beside her and turned on the lamp. "I should have recognized you sooner. Andy was right, you've had some work done. But you just can't hide those dead eyes of yours, can you Mallory? Or do you prefer Lila?"

The girl smiled. "I prefer Lila. Would you believe I like playing little diner girl at the Chick-N-Hen? It was almost like being invisible. But we'll have plenty of time to play catch up later. Right now, we're leaving. If you make a scene or try to get help, I will you shoot you and all your friends. Do I have your cooperation?" Lila flashed a gun at her.

Charlie nodded. She wouldn't put her friends' lives in danger. Lila led her down the hall and out through an old servant's entrance. She shoved Charlie towards the catering van.

"Get in the back," Lila commanded.

Charlie sat on the cold metal floor of the van. Lila rummaged through a gym bag and brought out some rope and a bandana. She got up in the van and grabbed Charlie's hands. She tied the rope tightly around her wrists and feet, then tied the bandana around her mouth.

"This should keep you out of trouble." She got into the driver's seat and drove away from the mansion.

Charlie was surprised when the van stopped just a few minutes later. The van doors swung open, and Lila stood there with the gun in her hand.

"I'm going to untie your feet, and you're going to walk slowly in front of me. If you try to run, I will shoot you. Do you understand?"

Charlie nodded. As she stepped down from the van, she tried to orient herself to her surroundings. It looked like they were on the far side of the lake in one of the few undeveloped areas. Lila directed her to a small cottage surrounded by overgrown woods. Once they got inside, she forced Charlie into a chair, tying her arms and legs to it. But she finally removed the gag. Lila sat in a chair across from her. For a few minutes, she just stared at Charlie, then the dead eyes finally came alive in an unbridled rage in her eyes.

"I've dreamed of this moment, sitting here as your judge. You should have been rotting in a prison cell all this time. But I'm here to balance the scales."

"Lila, I had nothing to do with planning your stepmother's death, but I didn't escape anything. I've spent my life regretting the affair with your father. I know it's what led to his actions."

Charlie never saw it coming. Lila leapt from her chair and slapped her hard across the face.

"Don't you dare lie to me! My father was innocent!" She screamed.

Charlie tried to regain her equilibrium. Her face stung, and her ears were ringing. She would have to be careful of her words. It was apparent now that Jack had lied to his daughter.

"Tell me what you know," Charlie said calmly.

Lila stood over her, fists clenched, but then slowly returned to her chair.

"Fine, if you want to hear your sins, I'll be glad to list them," Lila smirked. "Your freshman year of college, you seduced my dad. You didn't care that he was married, you were only interested in what he could do for your career. When you got the internship in Italy, you begged him to come with you. You had grown accustomed to the lifestyle he provided and didn't want to lose it. But he saw it as a way to finally get out of your clutches and wouldn't agree to go. In a fit of jealousy, you killed my stepmother and planted the evidence against my dad. But the detective in charge saw through your clumsy attempt and charged you, too. But you tricked the jurors with your wide-eyed innocent act. My poor father didn't stand a chance at his trial. So you still got your pound of flesh when he was sentenced to life in prison. Now, he's dead and his blood is on your hands too."

Charlie was speechless. Jack had managed to twist everything around, and in her mind, Lila was serving justice.

"So you found me here and used Kevin Wilson to blackmail me. Was the plan to kill him all along so you could frame me?"

"I'd been trying to track you down for years," Lila said. "On one of my leads, I found him in a bar outside of Waco. He was a despicable human being. That's when my plan began to form. I strung him along with promises of money until we found you. Blackmail was never my intent; it was just a way to keep Kevin on the string. Personally, I enjoyed making you suffer and would have liked it to have continued a little longer, but once you found him sabotaging the job site, it was over. You signed his death warrant. I got him real good and drunk that morning before work, then riled him up enough to go see you. It went better than I could have hoped. I loved standing there while I watched you dig your grave."

Charlie remembered now. Lila had delivered lunch that day. She had seen everything.

"But you couldn't have known I would go to his house that night or I that I would drop my gun."

Lila shrugged. "True. That was just a bonus. We passed your truck on the way back to Kevin's. He found the gun, and we figured it was yours. We went inside the trailer, and he never saw it coming. I did the world a favor by putting him out of his misery."

"What about Andy?" Charlie asked. "Why did you want to kill him?"

A dark cloud passed over Lila's face. "I didn't. I heard about the argument between the two of you while I was working. I had to make sure Andy didn't have anything incriminating on me as Mallory in his files. I didn't expect him to come back to the office that night. I still had your gun. When he came into the room, I shot him. I aimed to hurt him, not to kill him. My plan all along had been to plant the gun at your house and call in an anonymous tip. I had drugged your food that night, so I could sneak back in. Now it was even better, the police would link both shootings to the gun. I snuck back into your apartment, put the gun in your hands and fired it into a pillow so you'd have the residue on your hands, hid the gun and the hoodie, cleaned up, and then left."

"He almost died," Charlie said. "You have an odd way of treating the people you say you care about."

"You know nothing about me!" Lila shouted. "I loved him. He broke up with me that day I passed you on the road to his farm. He said he needed time to sort his feelings out. But once you're out of the picture, he'll come back to me. We had a connection."

"Is that why you set the fire at the storage facility?" Charlie asked. "Because he was at my apartment?"

"I wanted you to see your life's work burned down to ash," Lila sneered. "Andy is blind to what you really are, and now you've got Lance on your side, too. I won't let the system let you free again. I'm going to hand down your punishment myself."

"Do you think killing me is going to solve anything?" Charlie asked.

Lila smiled for the first time. "No. That's why I'm not going to kill you."

Charlie felt a sense of doom.

Lila breathed in Charlie's fear. "My father was a smart man, a wealthy man. You have no idea of just how rich he was. He had been hiding money from my stepmother for years and had the kind of money that can buy a lot of things, including a prison sentence. In the morning, you begin the journey to a new home. I hope you like a warmer climate. You'll be living out the rest of your days in some third-rate Central American jail. I've been assured you will suffer greatly, I even paid extra for it."

Charlie refused to let Lila get the upper hand. Instead, she began to recite the 23rd Psalm in her head. "Yea, though I walk through the valley of the shadow of death...."

She looked at her captor, twisted with grief, anger, and vengeance. Charlie could see herself in Lila's pain. She had been just as lost after she left California. She had been angry at God for abandoning her, ashamed of the affair, and devastated at the death of Jack's wife. Had it not been for her grandmother's love when she was at her most unlovable, how much different would things have been? Lila had no one except a father that had manipulated the truth, cultivated her rage, and driven her into darkness. The same God that had saved Charlie wanted to do the same for Lila. The cross didn't make exceptions.

"Lila, carrying out your vengeance isn't going to make you feel any better. The emptiness you feel right now will still be there tomorrow after I'm gone."

Lila shook her head. "You're wrong."

"Your father lied to you. He killed your stepmother, not me. He took advantage of your grief over your mother's death to help him get his revenge."

"Liar!" Lila screamed. "Stop talking!" She walked towards Charlie.

Charlie continued. "You don't have to be his puppet anymore. He's gone."

"I said, stop talking!" Lila slapped Charlie. This time, she drew blood.

"You can stop this. You can choose a different path!" Charlie felt the barrel of the gun against her forehead.

Lila gritted her teeth. Her hand shook. "You stop talking right now, or I swear you will never make it out of this room alive.

Charlie looked up at Lila, blood and tears mingling in her mouth.

"I forgive you. And all I can do is ask you to forgive me. My actions caused you pain. I was selfish. When I found out your father was married, I should have walked away. But I didn't. I loved him, and I thought that made everything right. I didn't think about anyone else but myself. And even though I didn't know about you at the time; it wouldn't have mattered. I pursued my happiness at the expense of others. You can pull that trigger; you can send me to that prison. It's not going to make you feel better. It's not going to take away the pain."

"You don't know anything about my pain," Lila lowered the gun. "But I will spend the rest of my life thinking of yours. You've not imagined the kind of pain you will endure for the rest of your life, no matter how short it is."

"Lila, put down your gun," Lance slowly entered the room from the back door.

"No!" Lila screamed. She pointed the gun at Charlie's head once more. "I will shoot her!"

"It's over," Lance said. "I can't let you hurt Charlie, but I don't want to hurt to you either."

Lila looked at Lance. Charlie took the opportunity to push herself forward in the chair. She aimed her head at Lila's mid-section. The hit knocked Lila to the ground and the gun flying across the room. Lance rushed over and cuffed the girl while she was still too stunned to move. A few more officers came running through the back door. Lance lifted Lila from the floor. She started screaming and cussing, trying to kick anyone that came near her. One of the officers finally got her out of the door. Lance leaned down and tipped Charlie's chair back upright as he untied her.

"Lance!" Charlie cried.

"Shhh, it's okay. You're safe. Let's get you out of here. There are some people mighty anxious to see you."

Thirty

Charlie refused to go to the hospital. She wanted the comforts of her own home, a hot shower, a cup of coffee, and to see Mr. Bear. Lance had called Andy, so everyone was waiting for her when she got there. Nan helped get her into hot bath and clean clothes. Her beautiful dress was covered in dirt, grease, and blood. After her bath, Wren and Susan applied some ointment to her busted lip and brought an ice pack for her face. Charlie found a fluffy robe and joined everyone else in the living room. Andy made coffee, and Charlie took a cup to her favorite chair. She snuggled Mr. Bear in her arms and cried into his fur, sobs racked her body. Andy rushed to her side, kneeling beside the chair. Charlie finally stopped crying.

"Lance, thank you for finding me," Charlie said. "How did you do it?"

"When you didn't come back to the party after a few minutes, everyone got worried, so Nan called me. I had just found the money trail, an offshore account that Jack kept hidden. It had millions in it and led to a real estate holding company that had purchased a lake cottage in the Cove. I was running the property against the recent arrivals matching Mallory's characteristics when Nan called. Lila Ewing's name came up as the resident at the cottage."

"I can't help but feel sorry for her," Charlie said. "I know she has to pay for her crimes, but her father took a young, grieving girl and twisted everything. He preyed on his own daughter to satisfy his vendetta against me."

Wren spoke up. "Let me give you some happy news. In light of recent events, the DA has dropped all charges against you!"

The room was filled with whoops and shouts and a bark from Mr. Bear.

"I can't thank you all enough," Charlie smiled. "Thank you for believing in me."

"Okay folks, our dear friend needs her rest, so let's pick this up tomorrow," Nan said.

Hugs and well wishes were exchanged as her friends emptied out of the apartment. Only Andy and Lance remained. Nan pointed to Andy.

"I'm staying the night tonight. I'm walking Lance to his car, so you have a few minutes, then you're going to let our girl rest too."

"Yes, ma'am!" Andy grinned.

Charlie hugged Lance before he left. "Thank you for saving me."

"I promise to never doubt you again," Lance said.

Andy took Charlie's hand. "I want you to get some rest. I'll come by sometime tomorrow, and we'll talk."

"Actually, I'm going to Pastor Richard's picnic tomorrow. I was hoping you'd come with me."

"Are you asking me out on a date, Charlie Flynn?"

"Well, last night doesn't really count since it ended in a kidnapping."

Andy smiled. "Then I will be here, and we'll see if we can get through a day without a murder, a fire, a kidnapping, or some other catastrophe."

"Deal!" Charlie agreed. "See you in the morning for church."

Charlie slept so soundly that night she almost missed the alarm. But she was ready by the time Andy arrived. They walked over together, and the first person they saw was Ms. Ada.

"My dear! Everyone is talking about your ordeal. I'm so glad you're safe."

"Me too!" Charlie said. "It was an experience I never want to repeat."

Ms. Ada hugged her and shook Andy's hand. "Mr. Brock, it's good to see you again. Please, both of you come sit by me."

The service was beautiful. Charlie asked to be baptized the following Sunday. After church, everyone gathered at the pastor's house. He was right, Virginia sure did know how to throw a party. Church members had brought along a dish or two as well. The afternoon was spent playing horseshoes, having an egg toss, and running a three-legged race. After lunch, a few people brought out their guitars and banjos, and they had a sing-along. Charlie had never been happier.

Close to dusk, everyone meandered toward the banks of the lake. Charlie and Andy sat on a blanket, waiting for the fireworks to start. Andy reached for her hand.

"You know, Moll, I've loved you ever since that day you pushed me out of the tree."

"Is that why you proceeded to date every girl in Holiday Cove except me?"

Andy laughed. "I said I loved you. I didn't say I wasn't an idiot. You terrified me. You were always so confident, so sure of yourself. When you left for California, I almost chased after you."

"Why didn't you?" Charlie asked.

"Fear. Fear you'd reject me. Fear you wouldn't. You're not the only one who's run from their past. I have a lot of regrets, but I don't want you to be one of them anymore. Now that we've both stopped running, maybe we can give this thing between us a try."

Charlie moved closer. "Counselor, I believe that's the best closing argument I've ever heard."

Andy grinned and wrapped his arms her. "I love you," he whispered in her ear.

"I love you too, Andy Brock."

Their lips met as the dark sky filled with an explosion of lights. They watched the display in each other's arms. Charlie's heart was full. She was finally home.

ACKNOWLEDGEMENTS

An author may write a book on their own, but it doesn't get into the hands of a reader without a lot of help. And this book is no exception. It was written during a very difficult time in my life. I had barely started writing it when I was diagnosed with Rheumatoid Arthritis, an Autoimmune Disease. There were days that I couldn't even get out of bed, let alone write. But I was blessed with friends and family who prayed for me, encouraged me, and never gave up on me. It is because of my faith and "my squad," this book is in your hands today. There are no adequate words to thank them.

Without my husband, Ken, I don't know if I would ever get anything accomplished. He is my rock. He has made many sacrifices so that I can pursue my dream of writing. He believes in me even when I don't believe in myself.

This book has gone through many hands before it's fit to be released. I tell my Beta readers to be brutal. They see things I can't, and I am forever grateful to them.

Every book needs a good editor and I have the best. Jeri Adams Ramsey, I don't know what I would do without you. Thank you for your generous spirit and your eagle eye. You make me a better writer.

As always, thank you to my family that loves me and encourages me daily. And I most thankful to the God that is the same on the mountain top as He is in the valley and that there is no "too far gone" in His eyes.

Dear Reader,

Thank you for taking the time to read this book. It has been a labor of love to write it. We are just beginning our adventures in Holiday Cove together. There are more people to meet and more mayhem on the horizon. Mr. Bear and I can't wait to visit with you again. Until then, you can keep up with us at **www.hmreaves.com**. See you soon!

62669361R00140

Made in the USA
Columbia, SC
04 July 2019